ISBN 978-1-330-57137-8
PIBN 10080241

1 MONTH OF
FREE
READING

at

www.ForgottenBooks.com

By purchasing this book you are eligible for one month membership to ForgottenBooks.com, giving you unlimited access to our entire collection of over 1,000,000 titles via our web site and mobile apps.

To claim your free month visit:
www.forgottenbooks.com/free80241

THE

HEN-PECKED HUSBAND.

A NOVEL,

BY

THE AUTHOR OF " THE M.P.'s WIFE."

IN THREE VOLUMES.

VOL. II.

LONDON:

THOMAS CAUTLEY NEWBY, PUBLISHER.

72, MORTIMER St., CAVENDISH Sq.

1848.

CHAPTER I.

THE early life of Theresa Dering is now before us; from the past history, from the sketch of the school in which she was nurtured, and from the peculiar nature of the soil on which the seed was thrown, we may naturally judge, with little difficulty, of the fruits which it will yield.

In a former part of her career, it has been

shown how Mrs. Dering thought fit to distinguish one daughter from another, by the respective names of Delf and China, and she was not singular in thus drawing a comparison between her children, for in almost every family, are we not every day eye-witnesses of this kind of distinction, even where the affection is just as equally distributed, as though all were held in the same estimation.

Georgiana Dering could not say,

> "I never was a favourite,
>   My mother never smiled
> On me with half the tenderness
>   That blest her fairer child."

for to give her her due, Mrs. Dering had never made Theresa the pet, although she made no secret of upholding her as by far the most superior.

Theresa knew from a child that she was beautiful, and she had been taught that upon that beauty rested her hopes for the future.

Georgina on the other hand had learnt, that the admiration which her face could not command, might be won by her voice, if she employed the "ten talents" entrusted to her charge, to advantage, and she did.

Theresa had domineered over her from a child, although she did not possess the *droit d'ainesse,* and this had rather subdued, and, strange to say, sweetened her temper than otherwise, without in the least diminishing the sisterly love which subsisted between them.

" I defy you to ruffle my Georgy," Mrs. Dering often said, and certainly she spoke on good grounds, for sometimes Theresa was enough to provoke a saint! but then

" Look in her face, and you'd forget it all!"

No one knew Theresa so thoroughly, as did her sister; no one gave her credit for such deep feelings, such warm impulses, and such firm, unchangeable affections, as Georgina did, and

it was this perfect acquaintance with her cha
racter that made her uncomfortable when she
heard of Mark Chetwode's acceptation, and
tremble as the wedding-day approached.

She trembled because she could not bring
herself to be certain that it would arrive at all!
She had heard, long before Theresa had, of
the altered prospects of Edward Sydenham,
and she felt convinced that if they reached
Theresa's ear in time, she would draw back
even at the eleventh hour, and throw up her
engagement, to the anger of her mother, the
despair of her intended, and the unquestion-
able discredit of herself.

Until therefore the letter, with the Dover
post-mark arrived, signed " Theresa Chetwode," Georgina could hardly be said to
breathe freely ; from that hour the weight was
off her mind, and she placed the letter in her
husband's hands with an expression of thankfulness, which he laughingly said brought down
her opinion of her sister's rectitude to a very
low standard.

" Not at all," was Georgy's argument, " I am only thankful that the impression on her mind which I had feared was so deep, was not unconquerable; I cannot think she would have actually married another if her feelings had not changed.

"Perhaps she never heard of Sydenham's not going with his regiment," said Mr. Keating.

" She *must!* I am sure she had heard it, though she never opened her lips to me on the subject, but I saw it in her face!—however she is safe now, thank Heaven!"

" *So far;*" interrupted the bridegroom-husband, " but if ever Sydenham comes in her way again, Chetwode had better look sharp."

This was essentially a man's sentiment—it found no echo in his wife's breast, for she had a better opinion of woman's sense of duty in general, and Theresa's in particular, to think that there would be the least danger in the encounter, whenever it were to happen.

The Dover letter said, the new-married couple were to cross to Calais as soon as ever the wind abated, but that Mark being a bad sailor, the sea, mountains high, had rather daunted him. The Keatings were of opinion that he would never make up his mind to cross at all! To expect the sea in November to be as smooth as a mill-pond, was expecting too much, and if Mark Chetwode waited for that, the chances were, that he would not come at all.

Georgina was one morning sitting in her pretty apartment in Paris, surrounded by her "belongings," and as quiet and demure, as though she had been married ten years, when the door flew open, and her husband suddenly rushed in, with the frantic haste which she now knew was habitual to him, so she had ceased to jump off her chair with fright at the banging of the door, as she used to do at first.

"They are come!" he cried, throwing open the window and going out on the balcony, "not ten minutes ago I saw Victor—1 knew the fellow in a moment, and he had a three-cornered note in his hand. They are come, Georgy, depend upon it! Theresa has triumphed and Mark Chetwode is by this time in Paris! if we have actually succeeded in landing him on French ground, we shall end by making him eat a frog!"

And at this moment the well-known figure of Victor really did appear, and as he glanced up at the balcony, the gesture of the hand which held the three-cornered note, intimated for whom it was intended.

How hastily it was torn open! how eagerly perused! and how impatiently Georgina waited till her husband had made himself what he called fit to be seen, to start off to Meurice's and welcome the bride and bridegroom.

Theresa was sitting alone, in the beautiful room they had engaged, when Georgina flew into her presence;—she was half concealed by the drapery of the window, and had not imagined her sister could have arrived so speedily, therefore Georgy caught the first expression of her countenance, which was peevish and inanimate, till it brightened up into delight at seeing who were her visitors.

Then came inquiries for Mark, for it was evident that extended on no sofa in the room, nor ensconced in any of the luxurious easy chairs, was the object of their solicitude, and Theresa begged Mr. Keating would go and see him in his own room, for they had had a fearful storm crossing to Boulogne, "and you know," added Mrs. Mark with an expression of face and a tone of voice which sent Mr. Keating off into fits of laughter, "*Mark suffers.*"

Yes, he had suffered dreadfully, and Theresa told Georgina that it was entirely his own fault, for that she had strongly advised their landing at Calais, whilst he had taken some idea into his head that though the passage to Boulogne was longer, it was not so rough.

" So we came in for the storm, and I thought Mark would have died."

" Nothing is so overpowering as sea-sickness," said Georgy, " and you Theresa?"

" Oh I am never ill you know, and I should not have been so provoked had it not been all his own obstinacy."

" But that cross sea to Calais—" began Georgina.

" Four hours instead of fourteen!—but it was against my advice, so how can he expect me to pity him?"

" Oh Theresa, surely no object is so deserving of pity as one who suffers from sea-sickness!"

" But it really almost served him right, poor soul! and in the midst of his agonies what do you think he kept saying to me?—' *My dear Theresa, I wish I could make myself more agreeable!*'"

Georgina would not laugh, though she saw her sister expected she should, and luckily Mr. Keating was not in the room. Georgy had

somehow or other imbibed a few very good
opinions and ideas as to the respect due to
the marital character, and she would not encourage Theresa in the faintest approach towards ridiculing her husband; even the very
tone in which the sentence regarding him had
been uttered, gave her a feeling of concern,
and she turned the conversation till the entrance of Mark and her husband, made them
look on the past in a spirit of merriment, and
the future, as one which they meant to enjoy
as much as possible.

"Well now what shall we do? where shall
we go? what would you like to see?" were
the first questions that hailed the stranger in a
foreign city. "Georgy and I have heard
every opera and every singer in Paris, but of
course, we are ready to go over it all again, for
your amusement."

"Too happy to find so good an excuse," said
Georgina archly.

So the carriage was ordered, and Mr. Keating went down to see it come round, for he knew all the circumstances, and was curious to see what sort of an equipage had been decided on.

His verdict was favourable; nothing could be more simple, and yet in better taste, and h congratulated Theresa on having discarded the cream-colour fantasy.

"You hear?" said she, turning to her husband, "you hear what Francis says!—are you better pleased? you know he is considered a good judge, and a man of great taste, so I hope you are satisfied."

Mark smiled good temperedly, and said he had been pleased and satisfied from the moment that he saw Theresa approved—at the same time, he could not say his eye was quite reconciled yet to the change.

"I am sorry to hear you say so," was Theresa's rejoinder, and then Mr. Keating exclaimed, "Never mind—he will improve in time," which remark was hoarded by Georgina till they were *en tête à tête,* when she entreated her husband to check rather than encourage her sister's proneness to laugh at Mark Chetwode, and oppose his tastes.

"He may bear it good-naturedly in the honeymoon," was her sentiment, "but the day may come when he will resent it, and Theresa is not one to submit to much control."

But Theresa had fortunately alighted on the very best ground in the world for being governed, for never were reins held with so light a hand as Mark Chetwode's.

His present life, as may be imagined, was very new to him—it was, moreover, one utterly different from any which he had ever led before —but still he saw that it was enjoyment to Theresa, and therefore he never murmured;— from morning till night he was in one vortex of excitement, and there was hardly a ball-room in Paris which did not claim and receive, at some hour of the night or morning, the eagerly-sought presence of the beautiful Mrs. Mark Chetwode.

In the day time, shops which she had once shunned for want of power to appropriate any of their glittering treasures, were now her constant resort, and her husband seemed never tired of suggesting first one thing, and then another, which he fancied would either please her fancy, or become her complexion.

Then in the evening at the balls! he was no dancer himself, but to stand in ambush, and watch Theresa's graceful movements was his greatest delight, for strange to say, in the whole course of his acquaintance he had never seen her dance!

The heavy eyes, the languid voice, and listless manner, which far from enlivened the breakfast table of the succeeding mornings, however, led Mark once to enquire if it were not paying rather too dear a price, thus to over-fatigue herself?

Theresa's answer was so sharp, that her

anxious husband never repeated his question; from that day he never remarked on whether she were doing too much or no, but silently waited in different corners of the gay rooms she was so fond of frequenting, and was ready with his patient smile to offer her his arm whenever it was her pleasure to exclaim, " Hold! enough!"

And so passed a month of their married lives, and Christmas was approaching with rapid strides, when, to the horror of all his listeners, Mark Chetwode coolly asked his bride one morning, what day she would like to fix on, for their return home?

Home?—Theresa raised herself in her chair with an air of unbounded surprise when the word was uttered, as if she hardly understood the meaning of it.   Home?   She gazed at her husband as though he had used some incomprehensible word, and said,

" Surely by 'home,' you cannot have any idea of leaving Paris?"

But that certainly was Mark Chetwode's idea, and he stood up firmly for returning home in time for Christmas Day, reminding Theresa that that festival was the following day week.

" I know it, of course," she answered, " but I also remember that to-morrow fortnight is New-Years day—the very best day of all the year in Paris—and one which I would not miss for worlds --would you, Georgy ?"

No—Georgina quite agreed with her sister that it would be impossible to miss that most enjoyable day, and Mr. Keating added that Mark would stigmatize himself as a perfect Goth if he left the gaieties just as they were beginning.

Notwithstanding, Mark was not to be moved, either by arguments or ridicule.   He had resolved to go home ; he had determined not to break through a rule which he had never yet infringed—of dining with his family on the Christmas-day,—and the more his wife argued, and his sister-in-law entreated, the firmer he stood his ground—it seemed as if nothing could move him, so remorselessly did he turn away his eyes, from first the beseeching, and then the indignant, glances of her whom he called his "gentle Theresa."

In vain she entreated—in vain she almost declared that she would not stir—the fixed smile on her husband's face provoked her far more than a frown, for it looked as if, for once, her wishes had no weight, and her words were of no avail; and therefore, no sooner had Georgina and her husband taken their leave, than she rose from her seat, and without a syllable, left the room.

Mark Chetwode sat down to his English newspapers, and having hardly observed that Theresa had departed in displeasure, was soon so deeply engrossed, that he entirely forgot the time, till, looking at his watch, he found it was nearly the dinner hour, and yet the carriage, in which he accompanied Theresa regularly every day, had never been announced.

In blissful unconsciousness of any mischief, a momentary thought crossed him that he must have been taking a nap, and he rung for Victor to ask, with apparent carelessness, if Mrs. Chetwode were gone out.

A sinister smile played upon Victor's features, as he replied that the carriage had come to the door, but that Madame had countermanded it.

Mark had chanced to look up in his face as he delivered this sentence, and the smile caught his eye—he did not like it, and he dismissed the man rather abruptly, but not before a something told him that all was not smooth, and he instantly walked direct to Theresa's room, and finding the door locked, requested to be admitted.

There was a pause before any answer was returned, and then it was merely an ungracious question as to who was there. His request repeated, met a still more ungracious reply.

"I have a headache, and am lying down;

if you have anything particular to say, I will rise and open the door."

He hesitated—he was "taken aback" as the saying is — and when he bethought himself whether he could conscientiously answer that he *had* "anything particular to say," he could not, for the life of him, recollect why he had knocked at the door at all !—therefore with a hasty entreaty that she would not disturb herself, he turned away, and taking his hat, walked out.

And now, for the first time, that indefinable feeling of uneasiness, which is one of the stages of latent disappointment, began creeping over Mark Chetwode, and he wandered backwards and forwards in the gardens of the Tuileries, wan and dispirited.

Every word that had passed between himself and his young bride that day, he now carefully turned over in his mind, and he could not recollect having used a single expression that could have caused the headache with which she had closeted herself in her own room.

He remembered that she seemed vexed at having to leave Paris;—that was natural enough, for he knew how attached the sisters were—and it suddenly occurred to him that the moment the Keatings had said good-bye, she had left the room herself in silence;—but why she had retreated so suddenly, so silently—why she had countermanded the carriage — and why she had answered his appeal for admittance to her presence so unkindly—all this was a mystery to him, and he drew his hat down over his eyes, and flung himself down on a bench, very much inclined to make himself miserable without quite knowing why.

In this state of disquietude, and from this state of sadness, however, he was soon aroused by a gay, careless voice at his elbow, speaking in those tones of levity which jar so unpleasantly on the ear when the spirits are not wound up for mirth.

"Decidedly, said the voice, "this gentleman is about to commit suicide or fight a duel; as he appears a stranger in Paris, and may want a friend, I offer myself as his friend!'

Georgina's merry laugh, as her husband pronounced these words, recalled the dreamer to himself, and he tried to laugh too.

"But why are you moping here?" continued Mr. Keating—"where is Theresa, and what are you going to do with yourself?"

"Theresa had a headache aud has not been out, and I fancy," said Mark, looking at his watch, "dinner must be ready—I have not dined—have you?"

"Bless your soul! dine in Paris at an hour when all the world are on the move to the different theatres?—Georgy and I are going to the *Varietés* go without your dinner for once, and come too?"

But Mark Chetwode was in no mood for so frolicsome an act; after a few more words he turned in the direction of his hotel, and left the gay young pair to follow their own devices.

" There has been a matrimonial dialogue there !" said Francis Keating, as they tripped gaily along ; " our bride has been flinging off a few airs and graces about returning to England, Georgina."

Georgina thought so too, but she thought more than she said about it ; she was curious to see what would be the result of this first difference, for evidently a screw was loose ; she was curious to judge how far Mark Chetwode would carry the struggle for the mastery, and whether he would stand his ground, or eventually give way, as everybody did, to Theresa.

" If he gives way," said Georgina, " he will lose the upper hand for ever ! I do not know which to wish, for if he is resolute, it will cost him dear."

" Better that than knocking under," returned her husband—" *ce n'ést que le premier pas qui coute*—after the *premier pas* it will be easy."

CHAPTER II.

DINNER was announced before either of the newly married pair had left their dressing-rooms, so they sat down to table without having had an opportunity of exchanging a word, but no sooner did Mark fix his eyes on the countenance before him, than he saw that the pale cheeks and swollen eyes betokened more than the headache which had been the reason assigned by Theresa for keeping her room.

Amongst the few things on earth on which Mark Chetwode looked with dread, woman's tears were the most formidable to him, for he had an inward conviction that if ever they were turned against him in the shape of weapons, he had not moral strength to withstand them.

Consequently he trembled for the moment when Theresa should open the conversation, for her brow was too lowering for him to hold any hope that words of sweetness would issue from lips, which were curling so ominously.

At last the moment arrived—the moment chosen being that of Victor's disappearance, and then, calmly raising her eyes, Theresa asked if he had decided on the day that they were to quit Paris?

The tone was so frigid—there was something so contemptuous in the voice in which the question was asked that it quite chilled Mark Chetwode, and he hesitated as he replied that as yet he had decided on nothing: he waited to talk it over with her.

Theresa laughed sarcastically.

" That is very good! when you told me that you were determined not to break through a rule you had never yèt infringed!"

" I said so, Theresa, before I knew or dreamt, that you would oppose a plan on which so much mutual happiness depends."

" May I ask for whose happiness it is that you are so considerate ? · What do you mean by mutual happiness ?"

" That of my mother, no longer a young woman, and myself; my dearest Theresa, is it so unnatural that I should wish to please my dear, kind mother, when I consider that perhaps she may not be spared many more Christmas Days, on which to see her family around her ?"

" I know nothing about that—I only see with pain and astonishment that my happiness is a secondary object with you! I see, (alas! just too late!) that the wishes of others are dearer to you than mine—in fact, that I am to be the slave of your will, and bend in implicit obedience to your fancies and customs—I thank you therefore for having taught me in one short month, the practical meaning of the most odious word in the marriage service—the word *obey !*"

" Theresa !" exclaimed Mark Chetwode.

He could articulate no more ; he was struck dumb !—he watched the curling lip, the flashing eyes, and the blue veins swelling on the fair and beautiful forehead in utter amazement at the sudden metamorphose, and he leant back in his chair, unable to utter another syllable.

Possibly had he retaliated, Theresa would have been daunted, but his conduct was so completely that which she had always been accustomed to meet, that she felt herself only too competent to continue the combat.

" Yes, and therefore I have made up my mind to act my new part to perfection; when are we to start? tell me the day and you will find me ready !"

Mark was irritated as much as so mild a

nature could be, by the tone adopted, and he coolly replied that the twentieth of the month would be soon enough.

Theresa did not expect this.

" Then you really mean to go ?" said she.

" Yes, since you consent," answered her husband.

" Nay!" she retorted, "do not call an ac- quiescence wrung from me, a consent! I ac- company you, because you command it."

" Not because I wish it ?"

" No, because I wish the contrary. You forget how ardently I wish to remain in Paris. You forget that Georgy's society is very pre- cious to me, now that our paths in life have separated; and also that I am naturally anxious to see mamma, and launch her in the excellent society in which we now move, before she takes up her residence in Paris, and places a gulf between us, perhaps for years."

Yes, Mark Chetwode agreed that all this was very natural—he did not in the least blame her for it, on the contrary, that they were praiseworthy sentiments; still that as she had now taken another name, and other ties, other duties were incumbent on her, and he trusted that on the present occasion she would accede to his request, and try and reward herself for the sacrifice she was making, by thinking how deeply and tenderly he should himself appreciate it and thank her, provided she complied with a grace which did not make it appear, as though she were doing great violence to her feelings.

Theresa said nothing; she had turned away her head, and was looking out of the window; he therefore rose, and on his approach she started up, but not before he had seen the tears, in large drops, rolling down her face.

This is what he had anticipated; this, what he had so dreaded, and the little firmness that was in his heart, melted away at the sight.

At that instant, Theresa was paramount,—Theresa's wishes, Theresa's will, and Theresa's tears were all-powerful, and in grieved and hurried accents, he entreated her to forget the past—to be happy—to assure herself that her will was his pleasure, and to rely upon it that since she made such a point of it, their Christmas should be spent in Paris'

The consent once given, the sacrifice made, and smiles restored, Mark Chetwode reflected on what he had done, and resolved within himself that he could not have done otherwise.

It was true that his mother would receive his excuses with regret and pain, but had he left Paris as he had so fully intended, he knew, from the experience of the last few hours, what he would have had to overcome, and he felt assured that it was better to incur, from his kind and considerate mother, the charge of being an over- indulgent husband, than run the risk of marring the enjoyment of Theresa in this early stage of their joint career.

Perhaps this sentiment was correct. At all events, even supposing it were a fault, it would have been one on the right side with most wives, and how was he, who had had so little experience in woman's ways and woman's wiles, to imagine that the violent opposition to his wishes, just displayed by Theresa, was much more the result of a systematic love of domineering, than any great anxiety on her part to spend the winter in Paris!

No; he had given way because he thought it would give her pleasure, and her gratitude repaid him a thousand times.

Theresa looked so beautiful that evening, when Georgina looked in on her way from the theatre, and when, taking his hand, she told her sister to thank him for his concession, that he fancied he had made no sacrifice at all!—he almost felt as though he had only gratified and delighted himself, in thus restoring smiles and sunshine to the countenance he worshipped, and the look and tone of triumph which his wife adopted whilst she uttered the words, was entirely lost upon him, though not upon those who were looking on.

"She has conquered," said Georgina, as she and her husband talked it over—"I thought she would!"

"Yes—and I am sorry she has."

"Oh Francis, you men want it all your own way!"

"Not at all—but in his motives for returning to England, Chetwode had the right on his side, consequently he should not have given way—I think he has acted unwisely, and if the concession of to-day is repeated a few more times, he will lose the whip-hand—at this moment Theresa has it."

And a few days after this, Mark was himself very much inclined to think that his compliance was unwise, for a letter, carefully worded, yet still full of regret and disappointment, arrived from his mother, in which she said that Mrs. Bellingham shared in the general sorrow at the

non-arrival of the bride and bridegroom, having
broken through her regular custom of wintering in Paris, solely to do honor to their
presence in London.

When Theresa had read the letter which her
husband had in silence placed in her hands, she
made no sort of remark, but calmly refolded it,
and gave it back to him, and thus wounded
him more than he had any idea he *could* be
wounded by her; it looked as though she
neither duly appreciated his kindness in indulging her, nor sympathised in his regret at having
disappointed those most dear to him.

He had yet to learn that his Theresa was a
despot—that her selfishness extended to the
exacting of all or nothing, and that even the
sorrowful air with which he had given her Mrs.
Chetwode's letter to read, had detracted considerably in her sight from the merit of his late
goodness!

But it was past now, and the subject was

dismissed, for the whirl in which they lived prevented its having its due weight, and now arrived Mrs. Dering.

As she had come unprovided with a lodging, it had been arranged by Theresa that she should take up her abode at Meurice's for a day or two, and then they could all assist her in her choice. Mr. Keating laughed heartily at this plan, and in a brief *tete-â-tete* with his brother-in-law, congratulated him on his guest.

" Hardly my guest," replied Mark—" merely staying at the same hotel, and if all those now resident there were considered as my guests I should have a tolerable party."

" And a tolerable bill—nevertheless, do not think you will escape the honour she has destined you, for I heard her tell Mrs. Norman not ten minutes ago that she was for the present on a visit to her son-in-law, till she found apartments."

" Really ?" said Mark, hardly knowing how to conceal a slight tinge of annoyance at the coolness of the proceeding—"and who is Mrs. Norman?"

"A great ally of Mrs. Dering's, and a very pretty woman, at whose house a bachelor may be very well amused, but where I would not allow even my wife's card to be seen!"

Mark's eyebrows contracted—"And a friend of Mrs. Dering's?" he asked, in a tone of surprise.

"Yes— bosom friend—nobody can say a word against Mrs. Norman, except that she prefers the society of our sex to her own—she bears a good enough name, *otherwise.*"

Mark shrugged his shoulders, and looked instinctively towards his wife.

Theresa was bending over the counter of a shop, in earnest examination, aided by her mother and sister, of a ruby velvet which her husband had requested her to choose as a present from him.

"Chetwode," said Mr. Keating *sotto voce,* "let me breathe a word into your ear—be

independent of Mrs. Dering's Parisian set—
they are all the Norman stamp, and if she
attempts to drag Georgy down into it again, I
shall leave Paris as fast as horses can be put to
the carriage! Now be warned by me, my
good fellow, for I have the key of most of Mrs.
Dering's mysteries, and when her two daughters were in the market, she cultivated every
body and anybody for the sake of society; and
as Mrs. Norman's house was the resort of a
perfect bevy of young men, she consented to
be almost the only lady of that fair lady's set
for the sake of speculation, and for the advantage of the girls; luckily, both escaped, for a
coolness sprung up."

"Why?" enquired Mark Chetwode, disgusted
at the recital, and fidgetting to get nearer his
wife, as if the very act of standing by so dangerous a mother were detrimental to her.

Mr. Keating hesitated, and the question was
repeated.

"Oh! some foolish womanly pique."

But this did not satisfy Mark; he pressed for a more explicit answer, and did not know whether to be pleased or annoyed when he gained it; Theresa, it appeared, had succeeded in drawing away two of Mrs. Norman's sworn admirers, and as they never returned to their allegiance, a coolness towards the fair thief sprung up.

On eliciting thus much, the husband wanted to hear more—who were these deserters? had they been encouraged to leave their former standard? what were their names?

" *Theresa* never encouraged them," said Mr. Keating, emphatically; " but I answer only for *her*; remember, too, that I have told you this, merely to warn you of the sort of society Mrs. Dering cultivated."

" But their names?" persisted Mark Chetwode.

" Wharton was one—Sir Henry Wharton—a great fool, and a great puppy, who got nothing for his pains but the anger of the old love, and the laughter of the new."

" And the other ?"

But Mr. Keating either was, or pretended to be, suddenly attracted by some one at the other end of the shop, and with a hurried sentence expressive of annoyance, he walked off towards Georgina, and hemmed her in between himself and a pillar, so that no one could accost her without his being complaisant enough to move, which did not appear probable.

The cause of this sudden manœuvre became apparent to Mark when he saw an affectionate greeting taking place between Mrs. Dering and a lady dressed with singular simplicity, and yet good taste; evidently this lady also was one against whom his crochety brother-in-law had some grievance, and he advanced towards his own wife to ask who it was.

Before however he had time to say a word, Theresa had hastily accepted some invitation, and was appealing to his taste as to the velvet dress, thereby engrossing his attention, as well as trying to prevent his asking questions—at least, so he thought, for the suspicious nature of Keating had infected him, and he resolved not to be baffled.

He therefore placed his hand decisively on the velvet, and saying that there was plenty of time for the selection by and bye, he wished to know before any further step was taken, what invitation his wife had been accepting as he joined her.

Theresa was surprised; there was something unusual in his manner, and in his eyes; there was a contraction too on his lip, which looked like determination, and she nervously answered that an old friend of her mother's had asked them to spend the evening with her, and as she knew they had no engagement, she had accepted.

" Without even referring to me ?"

" Good gracious, Mark! you know we have no engagement !"

" But who is the lady ?"

" Oh, a great friend of Mamma's; and such a pleasant house; and she is going to ask Georgy and Mr. Keating too—look, she has asked them. Look at Francis putting on a stiff face! he cannot bear her !"

In a moment it struck Mark who this lady was; he saw it by Georgina's cool manner and her husband's undisguised anger and annoyance—it could be no other than Mrs. Norman, and his mind was immediately made up to stand his ground *this* time, whatever opposition in the shape of wiles, tears, or indignation might be offered him.

He said no more then; he did not think it an opportune moment; neither did he say anything on their way home, for Mrs. Dering was in the carriage with them, but when Theresa went to dress for dinner he followed her, and on hearing a particular toilette ordered for the display of the evening, he no longer delayed issuing his veto to her joining the party to which she had been invited, having first, however, satisfied himself that the lady to whom his wife and mother-in-law had not considered it worth while to introduce him, was in very deed the Mrs. Norman, whose *unblemished* character, as sketched by Francis Keating, had so disgusted him.

Theresa's look, when the fiat left his lips, was a picture;—her expression of mingled surprise, doubt, and defiance; and when these conflicting feelings found vent in words, the torrent nearly overwhelmed the unlucky husband, and he wished himself out of the room a thousand times over.

" Francis has done this!" was Theresa's first exclamation when she saw that Mark was gravely determined that she should not be seen as Mrs. Chetwode in Mrs. Norman's house —" I am convinced he has been saying something to you! what on earth is the harm of my going? me, a married woman, to the quiet party of an old friend of my own mother's?"

" The harm is this—that though no one can point a finger at the lady in question, it is enough for Cæsar's wife to be suspected, and into that house, as my wife it is my earnest wish you should not enter."

" But what can you know of Mrs. Norman, Mark? you, who were never in Paris before? I am surprised at your taking gossip for gospel, and very much hurt that you should think mamma's friends not good enough for me."

" In this case Mrs. Dering has formed an unfortunate friendship; I am satisfied that the very fact of your having the *entrée* of Mrs. Norman's rooms would be sufficient to cause the doors of most other houses to be closed against you."

" Lucky mamma does not hear you," said Theresa, with a sarcastic smile.

" Perhaps she might thank me for initiating

her into what she may not be aware of; like a
game of chess, the lookers-on see more than
those who are playing."

"My dear friend," returned Theresa, with
an air and in a tone of infinite superiority, "if
you were speaking your own sentiments,
formed from your own observations, I might
pay more attention to what you say; but as it
is, I hear only the echo of Francis Keating's
ridiculous prejudices, and forgive you."

Mark half laughed at this forgiveness, but
he was not to be deterred from his purpose,
nevertheless. Though the appearance of Mrs.
Norman differed very much from the account
his brother-in-law had given of her, still it
was enough from him to hear a woman spoken
slightingly of, for his mind to be made up as
to whether his wife should visit her or not.

He therefore repeated all that he had said,
and turned to leave the room.

"One word," said Theresa, looking round—
"you have not been quite clear enough; are

you quite resolved not to go to Mrs. Norman's to-night?"

" Yes—quite."

" Not even if the Keatings go?"

" Theresa, you *know* they are not going!"

" But mamma is; and I asked her to dine and go with us."

" I shall be very happy to see your mother at dinner, my dearest, but you must ask her to be the bearer of a note of apology to Mrs. Norman as far as we are concerned."

Theresa paused for a moment, and then began again—

" How do you know Georgy is not going?"

" I infer it from a conversation I had with Keating; but my dearest Theresa, end this tiresome discussion; once for all I decline Mrs. Norman's acquaintance, and—"

" But if Georgy went, might I?"

Mark hesitated, and then said he was certain she would not; the pertinacity of Theresa annoyed him, and he answered petulantly,

upon which she laughed, and he was still more
vexed, for he thought it was no joke.

" Now, good, dear, man !" she at last coaxingly
exclaimed ; " do me a favour ! a great, great
favour—and you know I never ask favours
hardly—oblige me by just going to Francis
directly after dinner, and asking him if he and
Georgy are going to Mrs. Norman's—if they
are, fly back on the wings of repentance, and
let me dress for the admiration of all beholders;
if they are not, you may stay or come back
as you please, only say nothing to mamma till
you are quite determined—it is no use wound-
ing her feelings by cutting her friends, unless
it is quite unavoidable."

Mark assented—more because of her importunity than anything else—and because he was
so certain that from what Francis Keating had
said, there was not the remotest chance of the
objectionable invitation having been accepted ;
and Mrs. Dering arrived as usual, to dinner.

Her dress was just what it ought to have

been—pretty and dressy, but not out of character with the bonnet in which she meant "just to look in" at her friend's *soirée*. Her son-in-law never noticed the dress of any one except Theresa, and as he sat admiring her at dinner according to his custom, he thought she was looking more beautiful, if possible, than ever; perhaps it was that she had altered the style of her hair, and appeared in a shower of soft ringlets instead of her usual short, frizzy ones—at all events she was in great beauty, and he thought, considering she had been so anxious to join the party in question, that she had behaved very good temperedly on the occasion.

According to agreement therefore, as soon as dinner was over, he departed on his errand, having said nothing to his guest of the purport of his visit, and Theresa and her mother sat awaiting his return.

He went straight to the Keatings' apartments; they were out, but were expected home every moment, as they were going out that evening.

Mark was rather startled; could it be that Keating had been over-persuaded by his wife, just as Theresa had tried to over-persuade himself? and even if it were so, was that any reason that he should act in direct opposition to his own judgment, when that told him he was right in the course he was pursuing?

At all events he would sit down for a few minutes, and ascertain what their movements really were to be, and he waited patiently till about fifty clocks in the house had chimed their quarters three times over, and then he asked which way they were gone, and determined to pursue them.

To the shop indicated as their probable destination, he went; they were not there, but as far as he could make out of the voluble explanation offered him, they had left on their return home, about ten minutes, so he had missed them.

Secure now of catching them, he posted back again, and was this time fortunate, for Francis Keating was smoking out of the window, and Georgina attiring in another room, holding a conversation with him at the same time, when the wearied man arrived.

His mission was soon divulged, and soon answered. Mr. Keating first laughed at the idea of Theresa's imagining he would go to Mrs. Norman's, and then, more emphatically than politely, said where he would see her first; and as Georgina cried " For shame," from the inner room, she laughingly told Mark she thought it was a joke of her sister's!

" Theresa knows so well the antipathy Francis has to that poor woman, though really no one can tell what they have to say against her, except that she flirts!"

Her husband cut her short with his customary abruptness, and asked Mark if Mrs. Dering were dining with him?—" Because I have got a box at the opera, and if you and Theresa will join, we shall enjoy it all the more, but we do not want the old lady."

Having received an answer in the affirmative, it was arranged that Mark should wait a little while longer, so as to give Mrs. Dering time to depart to her *soirée*, and that then, he should take the Keatings' carriage, and hurry off for his wife, whose toilet was always made in the shortest space of time that any belle could well engross.

And so the minutes sped till the carriage came round, and Georgina being quite ready, said that she would go too, and wait for her husband at Meurice's, for she could then talk to Theresa all the time she was preparing.

They drove up to the door, both in high spirits, and they ascended to the drawing-room. It was empty.

"Theresa is in her room, I suppose," said Mark Chetwode, and he went to call her.

She was not there.—He returned to Georgina with an expression on his face which frightened her, and in spite of her hundred hurried questions, he almost tore down the bell rope before he replied;

" She is out," said he at last, as he breathed faster and faster—" where she is gone, remains to be proved—till I ascertain that point we will say nothing."

" But my dear Mr. Chetwode".......began Georgy.

" My dear Georgina," returned the agitated man, " do not speak to me just at this moment —I am not fit to answer you calmly, but if my suspicions should prove groundless, laugh at me to the end of my days."

Georgina was too terrified to feel any inclination to laugh—she felt far more ready to sit down and cry, for she was trembling all over; the picture of an angry husband cannot be viewed with indifference at any time; and to see Theresa's husband, the kind, good, and gentle Mark Chetwode, with every feature of his face set, as it were, into an expression, strangeness of which rendered it almost awful, frightened away every word that she wished to stammer out, so as to account for her sister's disappearance.

The door opened, and Victor entered.

" Mrs. Chetwode is out?"

" Yes, Sir."

" She accompanied Mrs. Dering?"

" Yes, Sir—to Mrs. Norman's."

The door was again closed, and at that moment the carriage returned.

Mark Chetwode folded Georgina's shawl round her in silence; when she looked up in his face and tried to speak, he silenced her by a glance, and she descended the stairs, and got into the carriage alone.

CHAPTER III.

"How rash! how wrong! how exceedingly imprudent, unless, indeed, it were thoughtlessness," were Georgina's exclamations, as they drove to the scene of their constant attendance and enjoyment, "what could poor Theresa have been thinking of to have so rebelled! for I really doubt if Mamma would have had the courage to set Mark Chetwode at nought in this way."

"Theresa is not thoughtless," returned Mr.

D 2

Keating, "and I consider the deep art she showed in getting him out of the way, was worse than the act itself; if I were that girl's husband, she should not be another hour in Paris !"

"My evening is spoilt," was all Georgina answered, and little sleep visited her eyelids that night, so anxious was she to learn whether the meeting between her sister and her angry husband had been stormy or not.

The next morning, though panting to start for Meurice's, Mr. Keating would not hear of her moving a step before the usual hour arrived at which she was in the habit of calling on Theresa, for he said her appearance and presence might look like interference between man and wife.

"Let them fight it out between themselves —matrimonial duellists should have no seconds and no witnesses, and the less you allow her to say to you on the subject the better, for she will only talk herself into thinking she is an

injured person; women always do; wives particularly."

" One would think your experience had been
very extensive," smiled Georgy.

" My own wife excepted," apologised the
bridegroom.

Before the hour, however, at which the
sisters were accustomed to meet, the appearance
of Mrs. Dering paved the way for arriving at
the whole truth without taxing the parties concerned, for their respective details.

Mrs. Dering was flushed, as if warm words
had been passing, and Mr. Keating, anticipat-
ing a very highly coloured version of the affair,
listened to her opening speech with a face on
which a smile and a sneer struggled for the
mastery.

" Such a scene, my dearest Georgy! and so
totally unexpected! for I give you my solemn
word of honor that till I returned home from
accompanying Theresa to Mrs. Norman's, I
had no more idea than the man in the moon

that it was Mr. Chetwode's wish that she should not go there!—thus, conceive my dismay when I suddenly found myself face to face with a man more furious than any being I ever saw, and subjected too, to the outpourings of his anger, when I was as innocent as an infant of any participation in Theresa's folly and indiscretion!"

"And when he found you had no share in it?"...cried Georgy, clasping her hands together with anxiety and impatience.

"Why, then he turned upon her—*of course!*"

"And still furious?"

"Yes, but calmer—more concentrated—and this morning the dispute re-commenced, and I came away, for really, though Theresa may have courage to answer for her own faults, *I* have not sufficient nerve to stand by, and hear her reproved for them."

"I must go—you will surely allow me to go to her," exclaimed Georgy turning to her husband—"no one can keep Theresa in order as

I can, and if she should be very intemperate, we do not know what the consequences may be."

Mr. Keating did not like it at all, but he did not demur much, for he felt with Georgina, that a serious dispute at this early stage of the married life of the Chetwode's, might lay the foundation for incalculable mischief, and if it were in his wife's power to throw oil upon the waters, she might go, and they all started together, though only one, the sister, entered the room where the husband and wife sat.

Before, however, Georgina went in, she had been waylaid by Victor, and much to her vexation, she found that he was quite aware of the stormy dialogue that was going on between his young mistress and his new master, for he plainly informed her that he was just coming to seek her when she appeared.—" Monsieur," he said, " was so exceedingly harsh with Madame—he had listened to his voice when its angry accents rose higher and higher, till he

bear it no longer, and he trusted now, that
Madame Keating would go in and interpose
as peace-maker."

Georgina did not like to blame the man for
his zeal on behalf of his young mistress; but
she was inexpressibly annoyed to think that it
was in his power to talk over the affair with
Theresa's very fine new lady's maid, and so
spread it far and wide;—she therefore thought
it best to exhort him to keep silence, assuring
him at the same time, that most likely it would
all end in a joke.

She lost his incredulous look, for the next
moment she had ushered herself into the drawing-room, but a new feeling—that of annoyance at the impertinent interference of Victor
—had sprung up in her breast, and she had
just time enough to feel, that in refusing the
services of the man of whom her mother had
made so much, and who had been for so many
years admitted to the united counsels of the
family, and made, in fact, quite one of them-

selves, her husband had done both well and wisely.

It has been said with much justice ; " *No tyranny like that of a servant!*" and perhaps Mrs. Dering felt this when she exerted herself so successfully to get rid of her "treasure of a man."

It is all very well to boast of the invaluable qualities of the " upper servant " who rules our household—(*and ourselves !* —though we would protest to one's dearest friend that it was not so—) we dare not do otherwise than extol their services, because to assert independence would draw down a mountain of discomfort on our heads;—nevertheless the shoe generally pinches somewhere, and had there been a window in Mrs. Dering's heart it would have been seen that Victor had had his day—she was beginning to weary of having him for ever at her elbow with his submissive face but despotic hand, and as he had held the reins of government so long, she knew that it was im-

possible to get them out of his grasp except by
placing him in some onerous situation elsewhere,
as responsible as her own had been to him
from the period of her husband's death.

An Englishman would hardly ever have
attained to the sort of power possessed by Victor;—it was the supremacy which in this country we see vested in the housekeeper, and Mrs.
Dering's own maid being a poor, weak creature, very deaf, very much attached to her
mistress and the young ladies, and an accomplished and indefatigable workwoman who
could copy almost any novelty which the dressy
widow pointed out to her observation on the
persons of her more wealthy friends, Victor
had had it all his own way. When Georgina
married he had just begun to say " Not at home"
of his own accord to middle-aged men a little
older than Mrs. Dering, who called oftener
than he considered necessary, and this had
frequently irritated her exceedingly—who can
say why ?—though she dared not show it;

nevertheless she played her cards well to the last, and transferred him quietly into the Chetwode establishment, having succeeded in making him believe, as she thought, that since the loss of her daughters, her " small means " no longer admitted of her keeping him.

It was all the same to Victor; his grim face smiled its customary smile of assent, for he, like his young mistresses, had also had enough of screwing, starving, and showing off, so he handed himself over silently, but he knew all the time as well as Mrs. Dering did, that Georgina and Theresa had not taken away a farthing from the income which the widow called her " small means ;"—he knew that they had neither of them any " *dôt*," for their plan-sible mamma had told him so a thousand times over, only she forgot it, like most people who romance, so his grim smile on the occasion perhaps partook a little more of sarcasm even than usual.

But a truce to digressions.

Georgina's unannounced entry silenced the voices that Victor had described as rising higher and higher, and the smile with which she was greeted by her sister reassured her.

Theresa was lounging in a *chaise longue,* and her feet were put up upon another chair in the most careless of attitudes, whilst her head was resting on the sloping back in so luxurions a position that she allowed the smile to do the duty of any greater exertion, except holding out her hand as Georgina approached, and languidly uttering words which had been better not spoken; they were—

" I am having such a lecture! I do not know whether your advent will interrupt my lord and master;" and a short laugh of derision followed, as the last expression was used with emphatic solemnity.

At a small writing table in a distant window sat Mark Chetwode, writing with rapidity, but he looked up when his wife spoke and begged Georgina to excuse his finishing his letter—after that he would explain.

" I suppose he thinks I am to sit mute," whispered Theresa—" but I shall do no such thing; I will tell you all about it, Georgy."

" Not a word," replied her sister, placing her hand on the scornful lips, " not a syllable, Theresa, till Mark is at liberty to attend; then, you shall tell your story, and I will listen, grieved as I am to have to do so, in a silence which means only condemnation of your conduct."

Theresa laughed!—she playfully doubled her fist, first at Georgina and then at her husband, whose eyes were on his paper, but at that moment he rose, and catching the action, gravely though mildly shook his head.

His first words were spoken more in a tone of sadness than anger; and Georgina felt that he was only acting exactly as any other husband would have done when he announced that they were about to return to England immediately. He added that he should only wait till his mother's reply to his letter satisfied him that it was convenient for her to receive them, and then he briefly alluded to the act of disobedience committed by Theresa the preceding night.

He spoke so moderately and sorrowfully of it, so differently indeed from what Georgy had expected, that she felt quite provoked with her sister and astonished at his temper during the running fire of little impertinences that Theresa kept up whilst he was speaking.

Throwing in trifling remarks—going through a by-play of alternate defiance and ridicule— and conducting herself with the utmost levity, was the young wife's present course, and Georgina kept her eyes reluctantly turned away lest even the expression of her countenance should in any wise encourage her in her ill-timed mirth.

" As to disobedience," said Theresa, amongst other rejoinders, " I plead not guilty, for you never told me I was not to go !"

" Theresa !" exclaimed her husband, astonished at the boldness of the assertion.

"I repeat it; you never did! you used the plural " *we*" the, whole time, and I honestly and candidly confess I crept thaough the loophole."

" Did I never say to you, Theresa, that into that house, as my wife, it was my earnest wish you should not enter?"

"If you did, I never heard you—besides, even supposing I acted wrongly, where was the necessity for flying at Mamma in the manner you did ?"

Georgina was thunderstruck !—what ? did her sister actually pretend to turn the tables on Mark Chetwode, and herself take the tone of the injured party ?

"I exonerate your mother," returned the

husband, "I exonerated her the moment I found that you, and you only, were to blame."

At this moment Mr. Keating made his appearance, and was greeted by the delinquent after much the same fashion as she had welcomed his wife.

"How do you do, Mr. Francis Keating?—are you come to see Sir Peter, or, Lady Teazle? because we are *two* to-day!"

"Oh! Theresa," murmured her sister.

"I come, not to take *your* side!" exclaimed her brother-in-law.

"No?—*et tu Brute?*' was all she answered, but her laugh, though louder, was now more artificial.

Very little more transpired at that time. Georgina obtained permission to take her sister out driving with her, and her husband went with Mark Chetwode; Georgina's hope and secret intention was, to try and prevail on Theresa to apologise for her misdemeanour,

but unfortunately the giddy heedless girl
thought that was the best joke of all, so the
laudable endeavours fell to the ground.

With Mark Chetwode and *his* companion,
the-case was very different. Cordially ap-
proving the firmness with which his brother-
in-law announced his determination of at once
removing Theresa from the scene of her rebel-
lion, Mr. Keating's abrupt manner and off-hand
remarks tended to strengthen the resolution as
much as anything, and his bluntly expressed
opinions had all their due weight on the wa-
vering mind of his companion, for he was just
the sort of person to gain an ascendancy over
Mark, merely by the careless way in which he
delivered himself of sentiments which were so
immoveable, as well as original, that they
seemed to carry their own power with them,
requiring neither the aid of repetition, nor any
other influence.

His emphatic advice was, that Mark should
lose no time, but start even the following

morning. Mr. Chetwode murmured something about lady's things taking time to pack, and servants being ready, in reply to which an insinuation was thrown out that there was such a word as "*must*," in an English vocabulary, peculiarly suitable to the present occasion. In short they parted mutually satisfied; the one that he had done his duty in urging the departure,—the other, that he was right in being for once firm, and proof against persuasion.

Meanwhile, Theresa was reclining in her sister's barouche, flirting with Sir Henry Wharton, who rode by the side of it, and telling him archly of the sudden commands under which she was to leave Paris immediately.

Sir Henry would not believe it; within a day or two of the festive time, he pretended to doubt that any "business in England," which was the plea advanced by Theresa, would make a husband take so barbarous a step.

Georgina disliked the tone of the conversation—she did not like her carriage either to be made the mark of observation, and she was not long before she gave the order of "Home," for she saw that nothing at that moment would please her sister more, than to encounter the two husbands, so that one should be annoyed and the other made jealous by the foolish game she was *acting*, not playing.

Just, however, as their cavalier had quitted his hold of the carriage door, they overtook their respective lords, and Georgina stopped to take them up.

No — they would rather walk, — and the carriage was again moving, when Theresa exclaimed,

"One word, Mark—when is it your august will that we go?—that we leave Paris for the dissipation of a London Christmas?"

"To-morrow," was the brief reply, and they drove on.

Theresa's lips were compressed. A look of determination filled those brilliant eyes, and she turned to her sister.

"Now Georgy—do you really think we shall go?"

" I do, indeed, Theresa."

" Will you lay a wager ?—gloves? -bonbons ?"

Georgy shook her head—she saw in Mr. Chetwode's face that he meant to be firm this time.

"Possibly—but so I do   too !—Georgy, I *will not* be treated in this way ! suppose I say I *will not* go."

"Why, then you will be taken."

" Six pair of white kid gloves, Mrs. Keating ?"

" No—not twelve pair !"

" A carriage full of bonbons ?"

" Not a ship load !"

" Are you quite incorruptible? then you throw me on my own ingenuity !—thank you for the agreeable drive ; and if you will be so obleeging, as Mrs. Bellingham says—*my aunt Mrs. Bellingham*—to call at the same time to-morrow, you will find me just as ready to accompany you as I was to-day!"

She sprang out, and ascended to their apartments. Georgina drove home half sorry and half amused, and though she earnestly hoped no dispute would arise from the defiance which her sister had so boldly announced, she nevertheless trusted, that for that high spirited sister's sake, the yielding husband would this once be true to his word, and insist upon that compliance to his will which his wife seemed so determined not to accord.

Straight up to her drawing-room went Theresa Chetwode, and before even looking round, she rang the bell, and Victor appeared.

Victor, with his ready step, did not keep her one moment, so that the resolve with which she had ascended the stairs had had no time to cool, and a few hasty words told him of the projected journey on the morrow.

The countenance of Victor testified no surprise;—it was too well tutored to exhibit any feeling whatever, beyond the submissive look which accompanied the " *Bien, Madame*" that he uttered, and it was then Theresa's part to assure him that all was not " *Bien* !"—that she had no intention of being ordered out of Paris in this way, and in short that he was to assist her to circumvent Mr. Chetwode.

" You know, Victor, we cannot be ready by to-morrow morning !"

" Madame, it is just possible"...

" But I do not wish it to be possible !" was her petulant retort—" you *must not* be ready Victor !"

Victor bowed obedience and smiled.

" You must retard everything—you must say it is impossible !—there must be no horses, or the carriage must want mending !—you must say in fact, that we *cannot* go !—Victor, do you understand me ?"

Again the bow of obedience, again the smile; this time it lighted up the whole countenance, and Victor was in his element. from that moment. Before he left the room, he fully comprehended what was required of him, and the amount of confidence which was reposed in him. Fully competent for the project in view, he felt once more re-instated in his old position; and had not a circumstance, over which he had no control, and which could not be foreseen, frustrated his well-laid plans, they would doubtless have been accomplished.

When Mark returned home, Theresa's placid frame of mind rather puzzled him—she seemed in the most perfect good-humour, and though he could not so easily forget his displeasure of the morning, and its cause, still her cheerful reception mollified, as well as mystified him.

He saw no symptoms of approaching departure,—no preparations for the hurried journey; and when Mrs. Dering glided in with the timidity of a person who is not sure whether they are in disgrace or not, and announced that she should not have the pleasure of dining with them that day, he looked at Theresa for an explanation—which, however, she did not vouchsafe, for she was seriously occupied in filling the compartments of a beautiful *bonbonnière* with the various purchases of the morning.

Silence between the bride and bridegroom! —stiffness between the married pair ere yet they had run two months of the race of married life together!

How did this augur for the years to come! how was the silence to be broken! and how the stiffness to be dispelled, and by whom!

Not by Theresa! for now she began humming a tune, and so plainly did her own bearing show that she did not consider she had been at all to blame, that her husband actually thought, or began to think, that she must entirely have mistaken him throughout; mistaken his injunction regarding Mrs. Norman's party, and his declaration that they should leave Paris the following day.

At last he spoke—awkwardly enough, but

still it served to break the silence. He asked
if it were possible that Mrs. Dering did not
know of their approaching departure? if she
were not aware that it was their last evening
in Paris?

" I have not told her," replied Theresa, in
the mildest of voices, " simply because I
thought it might embitter that last evening;—
beyond the pain of parting with me, our going
is nothing to her; it will not the least interfere
with her arrangements."

" But you appear to me to be making no preparations—you do not seem as if—".

" I have given Victor your orders—I considered that quite sufficient—as for *my* preparations, my maid will see to them."

" Victor, then, fully understands?"

" As much as I told him—that you wished
to start to-morrow morning; beyond that fact,
it was not my province to go."

Mark Chetwode was provoked at this new
tone his wife had adopted—if he had ventured

to be candid with himself he would have confessed, inwardly, that this sudden acquiescence
on her part made him feel more uncertain as to
her ultimate obedience, than even her refusals;
perplexed therefore as well as provoked, he sent
for Victor himself, positively determined that
there should be no mistake, but that from the
fountain head at once, the commands should
emanate.

When Victor entered, Theresa, being
seated behind her husband, could see the
changes of that remarkable countenance, and
make her own conclusions as to how far he had
carried out the orders which she had herself
issued.

No sooner had Mr. Chetwode spoken, than
Victor appeared at a loss what to reply—he hesitated—demurred—and at last expressed a
fear that all could not be ready in time, to
which his master promptly answered that all
must be ready !

Then came more hesitation;—if it had depended on himself, he should have taken no time in preparing, but he doubted if the Coachmaker would be able to send home the carriage so soon.

Theresa's eyes actually danced, as she gave an almost imperceptible nod of approbation, but Mr. Chetwode angrily demanded what the Coachmaker had to do with his carriage?

Now came Victor's triumph;—he thought Monsieur was aware that one wheel of the carriage had long been unsafe ; till that day there had been no opportunity of getting it repaired, and as, on that morning, Madame had said that she should not want to use it, he imagined it the best opportunity for sending it to the Coachmaker, who had said three days were required, before it would be safe as a conveyance!

" Foiled ! foiled ! and in the most unanswerable manner !" thought Theresa, and as Victor left the room, she looked meekly up in her husband's face, and said—

" You see, Mark, *homme propose,* but— "

If ever quiet human nature were roused to rage against its will, it was Mark Chetwode's at that moment! Foiled, he did indeed feel himself to be; foiled in his own sight, and stultified in the eyes of those, to whom he had so repeatedly protested his determination this time to stand his ground!

" This is your doing, Theresa," said he in a voice strange to her ears, " a continuation alas! well worthy the commencement!—but, though yon have placed the carriage beyond my disposal, another will serve our purpose equally well, and a hired one shall be the substitute for our own."

" You wrong me," was Theresa's answer as she rose to leave the room; " remember that it was only on my way home that you told me that to-morrow was fixed for our departure;— till then I of course imagined that according to your original intention, you would remain here till you received the answer to your letter to Mrs. Chetwode—thus, even had Victor told me *more* than three days were required to repair the carriage, I should have considered we had h e time to spare — you have wronged me Mr. Chetwode, and I see you know you have !"

And Theresa vanished, having contrived once more to make herself appear the injured party, and leaving on her husband's mind an impression that he had acted unjustly towards her !

That the injustice (?) was attached to only the events of the last few minutes, mattered little—it was enough that the impression had been left; and when those two met an hour afterwards at dinner, Theresa was the amiable and forgiving victim, and Mark Chetwode the harsh and hasty husband !

CHAPTER IV.

REPENTANT, inasmuch as regarded the circumstances of that last hour, but not otherwise, was Mark Chetwode.

He had been roused, and the resolve had been fixed thereby, but certainly the beautiful expression of sadness on his wife's face, as she sat opposite to him, like an accusing angel, touched the tender corner in his heart, and made him wish to himself, (what he would not have imparted to any soul) that he could find any, fair excuse in the world for staying in Paris—any little practicable *ruse* by which he might pretend he was detained !—in short, any innocent white lie which might cloak his relenting spirit, and suffer him to indulge the creature who had so artfully wound herself round his affections !

But it was not to be ;—he was pledged to go, and go he must ; and he certainly thought Theresa had behaved very well in submitting with so little trouble.

In this spirit, then, they sat at dinner together, and but few words passed between them ; the presence of Victor operated like a sort of spell upon Mark, and he felt a difficulty of utterance before him for which he, would have been unable to account even to himself.

Strange to say, that silence never creeps in between any other relations in life—it belongs exclusively to married people, and it grows

upon them day by day, and year by year, unless actively opposed and strenuously guarded
against.

To such a state, Theresa and her husband
had not yet quite come, but they had arrived
at a stage not very far distant—a stage of silence during the presence of their domestics.
both feeling equally that they could not talk
on indifferent subjects, and that therefore they
had rather not talk at all.

In this mood, the dinner took its course, and
finally concluded. Mark then drew his chair
to the fire, and Theresa threw herself on the
sofa and closed her eyes, occasionally peeping
through the long lashes to see if her indifference
had any effect on the insensible being before
her.

But Chetwode's attention for a wonder was
not, just then, with her. Her wiles and her
witcheries were alike lost upon him at that
moment, for his thoughts were diving down
into the abyss of futurity, and he was won-

dering to himself whether she who had thus proved herself disobedient in the green tree, might not end by being rebellious in the dry.

There was nothing on earth he loved as he did Theresa—his affection for her was all the more vigorous because it was a novel sentiment —and he would have done anything in the world to please her, or to make her happy; consequently her apparent disregard of his own happiness jarred painfully on his feelings and made his heart sink with vexation and disappointment.

Alas! alas! how soon to be disappointed! what a "little day" had the dream lasted! not two months had elapsed since his marriage, and yet already the sighs he was breathing were laden with fear and distrust for the future.

Whether that evening would have ended in a reconciliation or not, cannot be told, for before the heavy moments had melted into an hour, Victor marched into the room with a note in his hand, and placing it before his master, waited like a statue for the reply.

Theresa watched her husband's face, for she could glean nothing from Victor's, and the varied expressions that passed over it were partly explained when he suddenly ejaculated,

" From my aunt Bellingham! no answer—I will answer it in person."

Theresa rose—Mrs. Bellingham in Paris?— she who was to have formed one at the Christ- mas parties in Hill Street, actually false to her allegiance there, and true to her old quarters in the centre of gaiety?

" Do you mean to say," she asked, " that Mrs. Bellingham is actually in Paris?"

" Yes—the note is from Mary Vere—my aunt never writes—but she says, that hearing we had given up our intention of wintering with my mother, she instantly started to ... to enjoy our society here."

Mark had hesitated, because he knew that that courteous phrase was composed by Mary Vere, and that, in fact, it was much more likely the old lady had come for her own pleasure and convenience,· than for any gratification to be derived from the company of her newly-married nephew and niece.

" And you are going to answer the note in person, you say ?"

" Yes—she wishes to see me"—and as Chetwode pronounced the words, he screwed up the note, and tossed it into the fire—an act which convinced his sharp-sighted wife that Mrs. Bellingham wished to see him, and him *alone*, otherwise he would have showed the note.

" Then I suppose I may spend the evening with Georgy —*our last evening* you know."

The emphasis on the words was so provokingly marked, that Chetwode felt quite called upon to notice it, for though Theresa's lips asked no questions, her eyes did, and he had an inward conviction that she knew or guessed, as well as he did himself, that his aunt's arrival would, or might, materially alter their plans.

He felt in an uncomfortable position just then; though the pretext for remaining in

Paris, for which he had been wishing, had now actually arrived, it had come in the wrong shape; the alteration in his plans would now make Theresa think, and with some justice, that what she had begged and entreated for in vain, was to be instantly accorded by one word from " my aunt Bellingham," so Mark both stammered and turned away when he answered.

" By all means...very natural...I will leave you there myself, but it is not impossible that that we may stay over to-morrow"...

" More probable than impossible," were Theresa's parting words as she left the room to put on her bonnet, and unfortunately Mark felt that she was right—he was certain they would not go the next day!—and now he had to go and spend the evening with his aunt, she who would sift, as she ever had sifted, his every word, look, thought, and intention, and he would have to act his part as well as he could, for *act he must!*—how could he tell her that a

bone of contention had already sprung up between himself and his perfect Theresa? how
could he tell her that that being whom he had
represented as so gentle, so yielding and so
obedient, had already boldly defied him and
openly disobeyed him?"

At the former Mrs. Bellingham would smile
—and such a smile as hers was!—at the latter
she would triumph, because she had predicted
it, and there is nothing on earth that the fallen
hate so much, as any communication with those
who foresaw their fall.

Who is there who cannot fully enter into
the disagreeable sensations roused by the ob-
noxious sentences " I told you so!—" I was
sure that would happen!"—" Just what I pro-
phesied from the beginning!"

No—Mark, the open, the honest, and the
simple hearted, must now begin to weave webs,
and frame neat little falsehoods, and whilst ac-
knowledging to his own conscience that the

painful necessity was unavoidable, he " laid
the flattering unction to his soul" that he did
it *for Theresa's sake !*—All must be smoothed,
all concealed, all forgiven and all forgotten, *for
Theresa's sake !*—and by this time she herself
appeared equipped for the evening expedition,
all smiles and all sweetness, for so charmed was
she at having to tell Georgy that they were
not going the next day, that she quite forgot
the accidental means by which her end and aim
had been gained.

Georgina expected her sister, so her appearance excited no surprise ;—Mr. Keating did
not even look up from the difficult passage he
was executing on his eternal flute, therefore
Theresa stopped up one end of it with her
finger to arrest his attention.

" Listen to me, Francis—forget that beloved
instrument for one moment if you can, and do
you and Georgy both listen to me—I am come
to drink tea with you."

" I see you are come, and if to tea, where is

Chetwode?" returned her brother-in-law impatiently.

" Gone out to tea too—never mind where— if *I* do not mind, of course you need not;— but I was going to tell you what I came for besides my tea—"

" To make me waste my time, evidently !"

" More likely to save you from a fit, into which you will most certainly puff and blow yourself one of these days—but it was for neither of these purposes—I came to claim from Mrs. Francis Keating six pair of long white kid gloves, as many *bonbons* as a five pound note will purchase, and a drive in her carriage to-morrow at two o'clock precisely !"

Georgina and her husband were both really astonished. At first they could hardly believe but that Theresa was joking, and when they found this was not the case, the pleasure with which they hailed her detention was mingled with much unfeigned regret at what they supposed was the result of her wilfulness, and her husband's weakness.

"How was this achieved?—what has happened?" were natural questions to which Theresa ¦did not choose to give any direct answer; she would not suffer the brief hour of apparent victory to be dimmed by the confession that circumstances totally unconnected with herself had wrought the change of plans, but spent that evening noisily, and merrily, alternately amusing and annoying her brother-in-law until finally called for by her husband.

Mark Chetwode's evening had in the meantime been very differently spent.

Depressed by the events of the last day or two, and unhappy at heart, he entered Mrs. Bellingham's rooms with an assumed vivacity so foreign to his nature that it instantly caught the inquisitive eye of his aunt, and his forced spirits sat so awkwardly on him that she saw in a moment he was acting a part for some unknown purpose, and consequently resolved with all the energy of a very enquiring mind, to discover the cause of his singular metamorphose.

Her first questions, as a matter of course, were concerning Theresa; and when they had been satisfactorily answered, she expressed herself grateful to the young bride, for having spared her the advantage of her nephew's society for a few hours.

" Not many young brides would have consented to be left alone to gratify an old lady's whim," was her observation, and then Mark had to say that Theresa was not alone—that she was gone to drink tea with her sister,—in fact that until Mrs. Bellingham's unexpected arrival, he had thoughts of leaving Paris the next morning.

" Leaving Paris ?" repeated the old lady, turning her best ear towards him and scanning him at the same time with the most searching glance; ." my good man, what is come to you?

—did you not write and tell your mother that you intended spending Christmas here?—thereby disarranging all her plans and all her parties, besides effectually putting *me* to the rout, which I suppose you think a very secondary consideration! Do you mean to say you never wrote that letter?"

" No; I did write that letter certainly, but I have written another since, saying that my plans were altered, and that I should still hope to be with her if not by Christmas Day, certainly by New Year's!"

" And pray what has made you so shifty all of a sudden?" persisted Mrs. Bellingham.

" Circumstances," said Chetwode, "which I thought would oblige me to go to town, but now that you are arrived, I have a great mind to stay."

" Nay! don't make me the excuse for shifting and changing again, for goodness sake! nothing I hate like whimsical people."

" But this is not all whim, my dear aunt;

you must consent to patronize us for a few days at all events, for something has gone wrong with the carriage, and we cannot move at present."

" What! that fine new carriage of yours? ha! made of gingerbread, no doubt! Better have kept to the old maker, even if you could not put up with the old colour."

"My dear aunt, it was you yourself who named to us all the first builders in London, one of which we chose; but this is nothing of a break-down; only some slight injury; and if you insist on our going the moment it is rectified, we shall see nothing at all of you."

To confess the truth, Mrs. Bellingham had anticipated with no small satisfaction the pleasure of taking so beautiful a girl as Theresa into some of her " good houses," therefore before they parted she had arranged with her nephew to call for his wife the next day, and take her with her on a tour of distinguished visits.

"And how have you amused yourselves
here?" was her next question; what have you
been doing, and where have you been? How
have you felt in the new world? like pelicans
in the wilderness I suppose!"

"No indeed; we have seen everything, and
been very gay too—at least all seems gay to
my unaccustomed mind."

"Who do you know to be gay with?" said
the old lady, sharply: "I thought you were
not acquainted with a soul in Paris; surely
you have not got into Mrs. Dering's set?"

"You forget you gave us several letters,"
returned Mark; and stung as he was by the
scornful term by which the friends of his
wife's mother were designated, he felt too
much like a culprit to reply to the last part of
her sentence; he therefore quickly turned it
off by adding, that they had also been a great
deal out with the Keatings.

So passed the early portion of the evening,
and Mrs. Bellingham could not, by all her

cross-questioning, discover whether her nephew were in reality the perfectly happy man he had expected to be, or not. She did not understand either his joking humour or his constrained one;—she could not quite decide which of the two were assumed, but she suspected that both were, and so clearly did Chetwode perceive that it was impossible to deceive her entirely, that every moment only added to his discomfort and increased his awkwardness.

The fact was, his aunt's warning, breathed before his marriage and till then forgotten, now began echoing in his ears, and recurring to him in spite of himself, and he positively dreaded every approach to Theresa's name, lest the fact of his yielding kindness to her, and her influence over him, should ooze out, and bring down upon his head again the accusation of being a " Hen-Pecked Husband."

Above all things, he dreaded most, that Mrs. Bellingham should become aware of Theresa's having been to an evening party at Mrs. Norman's.

In the event of this coming to her ears, what was he to say?—If he allowed her to think that it was with his sanction, how was he ever to defend himself against the torrent of censure which he knew would be showered upon him for such a glaring want of judgment and discretion? If he said that it was without his sanction?—no, he could not own [that, for that would be worse than all!—rather than allow Theresa to appear in a disadvantageous light before his nearest relation, he would incur anything and everything! So when his aunt went on questioning him about his acquaintances, he nerved himself up to answer her carefully and cautiously—to be in fact as "wise as a serpent," and yet "as harmless as a dove" and to give no voluntary evidence whatever.

And now the evening, like all things both

agreeable and disagreeable, came to an end, and Mark hardly gave the clock time to strike the decent hour for retiring, before he started up, and declared that Theresa would be waiting for him. He was so rejoiced to be emancipated, that Mary Vere, in her boundless romance, thought his impatience was the most beautiful trait of devotion in the world—she had no doubt but that it had been his first separation from Theresa, and she thought his anxiety to rejoin her quite touching.

Mrs. Bellingham, too, was lost in thought when her nephew took his departure, but her train of fancies did not run in so high-flown a vein, and her mind was only dwelling on the wondrous change which a few months could effect in the most unsophisticated being in existence.

Mark was changed—so changed, that had his looks and voice participated in the metamorphose, she never would have known him again.

The very expression of his face was not the same, for no countenance could have been more open and honest than his once was, and now there seemed a sort of veil over it—just as if he did not chose her to read what was passing within.

"In short, Mary Vere," said she, before wishing the final good night, "Mark Chetwode was a bachelor too long before he married—marriage has routed up all his old habits—the man repents already, and I saw it at a glance!"

Had Mrs. Bellingham seen her nephew hurrying towards the Keatings' after he left her, briskly and cheerfully, perhaps she would have retracted this expression; he was another creature then, rejoicing in his freedom, and longing to see Theresa's pleasure when he told her that they were really going to remain a little longer in Paris.

Full, then, of this anticipation, he was not a little damped when, on entering the family group, he was greeted with,

" So you are not going to-morrow after all !"

One does not like, when one has secretly resolved upon some scheme, which is to be productive of great satisfaction, to find that the news has preceded us, and that we are thus shorn of the small amount of merit which we had awarded to ourselves.

Mark felt this, and yet before her brother and sister he did not like to tell Theresa that she had been rather premature, and so he let it pass.

This trifle, though such a very trifle, was but another trait in his nature and his character; too inert as regarded his own interests and too idle to assert points connected with his own dignity, he thus let slip opportunities, which, though insignificant in themselves, were still of sufficient consequence when heaped one upon another, to sink his authority in the scale and place him on a secondary footing, whilst Theresa took the lead as the influencing

cause of all their movements and silently assumed a power to which she had no right.

As they drove home, he took the first opportunity to tell her of Mrs. Bellingham's inteu-
tion of calling for her the next day and begged
her particularly to say nothing of her renewed
acquaintance with Mrs. Norman unless his
aunt questioned her so that she could not
avoid it.

To this injunction Theresa made no reply
but to Mrs. Bellingham's invitation to drive
she instantly gave an unhesitating negative.
She had promised to go out with Georgina,
and nothing would induce her to break her
engagement, because they had agreed to enjoy
the afternoon somewhere or other together, and
Georgy would be disappointed.

By this time, however, Chetwode had begun
to know his sister-in-law; he knew that she
always took his side in matters of this kind,
and he was sure in the present case she would

for once forego an afternoon's amusement, when she learnt his reasons for requiring it.

Not so Theresa,—she would not even hear of Georgina's being appealed to. An ancient dislike to Mrs. Bellingham, added to no small portion of pique that she had not been included in the invitation to tea that evening, made her only more resolute in her negative, and she closed her eyes in sleep that night, assuring her husband that another day would do quite as well for his aunt, and that no day in the whole course of the year would so completely suit Georgina and herself.

Mark saw through this; he was not now blind to his wife's defects, though in his mild phraseology, he termed her obstinacy and wilfulness the thoughtlessness of a spoilt child; and still hoping to prevail on her to accede to his request, he suffered the subject to rest till after breakfast the next day, and then it was renewed.

F 2

" My dearest Theresa, how seldom I ask anything of you that I see you dislike! for this once, therefore, indulge me, and write or send an excuse to Georgina in favour of my aunt Bellingham."

" Not for worlds, Mark! my aunt Bellingham, depend upon it, does not care one straw whether I go with her or not; it was only a little piece of politeness to you."

" On the contrary, Theresa, she did not even invite me to be of the party—she simply wished to present you to some old and valued friends."

" Stiff old people born before the flood, I dare say! no, Mark; you know I never should please them, for I hate that sort of society, therefore why put me in the way of making myself disagreeable? tell the old lady when she comes that I had a previous engagement to Georgina—you know I shall have a good hour's start, for Georgy calls for me at three,

' so there will be no scene of single combat!'"

"Could you not take the hour's drive, and return in time for my aunt?"

No; no arrangement would satisfy Theresa, and her husband was excessively provoked. In vain he represented to her the crochety nature of his aunt—the submissive deference which every member of his family had been in the habit of paying her, and the kind and warm-hearted being she could be if a little indulgence or consideration were shown to her peculiarities. Theresa listened to his harangue with a careless smile, and he had the mortification of perceiving that it had not made the smallest impression. She was just as determined at the close of it, to keep her engagement with Georgy, as she had been at the commencement, and it ended by Mark's writing a note, and explaining to Mrs. Bellingham that Theresa had so entangled herself in an engagement that she was obliged to decline going out visiting that afternoon.

When this note reached the old lady she was not well pleased; she did not think it "the right thing" that Theresa should make engagements without her husband's knowledge, which were too binding to be broken; Mrs. Bellingham thought her too young for such free agency, and she made a note in her mind to speak to Mark on the subject the first opportunity.

She then proceeded to scatter her cards about in different directions, and Mary Vere as usual sat in the carriage, wherever Mrs. Bellingham got out, and took charge of the precious Mimi.

Thus occupied, and amusing herself with improving the ringlets that clustered on Mimi's graceful ears, Mary Vere was suddenly aroused by a greeting from Sir Henry Wharton, who was going to call on the same people on whom Mrs. Bellingham was at that moment inflicting a sitting.

She was pretty and entertaining enough in her

way to arrest his steps, and as he leant on the carriage door they began chatting over the different parties and people of the set in which they mutually moved.

At last, naturally enough, the Keatings and Chetwodes came on the tapis, and the sensation Theresa had created was commented on as a matter of course.

Sir Henry had met her constantly in society —the Keatings he had not met so often.

" They live so much amongst musical people, and musical evenings are intolerable bores; Keating is a very good fellow without his flute, but to be always running up against a man who would rather go out without his hat than his music, is too much of a good thing; however Mrs. Keating sings more divinely than ever, and sometimes I victimize for the sake of her delicious voice."

" And that good, excellent Mr. Chetwode?"

" Oh, the excellent Chetwode is as excellent

as ever—more so, perhaps, for never was a more submissive, obedient, and indulgent specimen of humanity;—we think here that the order of the marriage service was reversed for that occasion only, by particular desire; and when you see them together you will own that he rigidly keeps his vow to ' love, honor, and obey !' ''

Mary Vere looked anxiously towards the door from whence Mrs. Bellingham would issue, fearful lest she should overhear what would certainly make her more sour and cross than she usually was even, but the old lady was not yet in sight, so she hazarded the innocent question of whether Mrs. Mark were looking well?

" Beautiful !" was the reply, " and infinitely improved by not adhering so religiously to the fashion of the day in the style of her hair; instead of those odious—yes, odious even in her !—those odious crêpé ringlets, which always remind me of a thousand spiders' webs in a tangle, she sports real ringlets, not unlike those of a fair lady who shall be nameless!"

Mary Vere's giggle rose hysterically as this compliment passed, and Sir Henry continued:

" She appeared for the first time in the new arrangement at Mrs. Norman's the other night—and only imagine—unattended by Cerberus!"

" Mrs. Bellingham," exclaimed Mary Vere, hastily, and wheeling round, Sir Henry made way for the old lady, and caught her sharp eye fixed upon him with a severity which he did not know how he had deserved,

Mary Vere knew!—she knew that his last words had been heard, and that Mrs. Bellingham's horror at the discovery she had made so accidentally, would very, very far exceed even her own, for by force of habit the humble companion had learnt to make all the feelings and sentiments of her benefactress her own, and therefore the announcement of Theresa Chetwode's having been alone to a party at Mrs. Norman's filled her with surprise and dismay, and she awaited the opening of the old lady's lips in mute and anxious awe.

" FLIRTING as usual!—flirting and frittering away your time!" were however the first words—" never can I leave you alone for one moment but I find you have picked up some one to talk nonsense to! Mary Vere, when will you leave off being such an idiot?"

The relief of this commencement was very great; indescribably so to the pretty goose to whom it was addressed, for she was one of those amiable beings who would infinitely rather have

the storm directed against themselves than
against any one whom they valued, and Mary
Vere from her infancy had been taught to re-
vere Mark Chetwode, who had on his part been
a kind friend to her through life; she therefore
satisfied herself with assuring Mrs. Bellingham
that she had not been flirting, and that Sir
Henry had only paid her one compliment—and
that was a very small one—merely about her
hair.

" What was the man saying then when I
came ?—do you pretend to say he did not mean
me when he spoke of Cerberus ?"

" Indeed, dear madam, he did not !"exclaimed
Mary with thoughtless haste, and then she
stopped suddenly for the next question placed
her in a difficult position.

" If he did not mean me then, who *did* he
mean ?"

And then there was no evading the answer—
out it must come—Mr. Chetwode, the good,
the grave, and the dignified, was the person

whom the trifler had ventured to designate by the title of Cerberus!

This answer of course led to other questions, and at last, piece-meal, the whole was elicited, and Mary Vere had the gratification of perceiving that she, who though always endeavouring to speak the truth so as to make the best of any bad case, had entirely succeeded in putting Mrs. Bellingham into one of her most towering passions, and exciting her anger and indignation against every soul concerned, from her unworthy nephew who had been so deep and designing, down to the humble companion herself, Mrs. Dering, Mrs. Keating, Theresa, Sir Henry Wharton, and Mrs. Norman, inclusive.

After the first burst, however, a question arose in her mind as to whether it could possibly be true that Mark had allowed his young wife to go to the house of a person who was not at all in society, without him?—not that Mrs. Bellingham knew anything particular against Mrs. Norman—nobody did—but she was not in society, and that was quite crime enough;—could it possibly be true?—had Theresa indeed so much influence as to do whatever she pleased, and go wherever she liked? Of course she had gone with her mother, for every one knew that Mrs. Norman was Mrs. Dering's friend, but even that did not palliate the offence—Mrs. Bellingham was convinced that it was all a deep plot of Mrs. Norman's to get a Chetwode into her house, or at all events to show off so attractive a bait at her evening parties, so Mark must be summoned to be questioned, reproved, and laden with the burden of the united sins of the whole party.

Whilst this was passing, Chetwode himself was taking a solitary walk, as unconscious of where he was going in that great and gay city, as if he had been suddenly dropt down upon Mount Hecla.

Not feeling in spirits to accept Georgina's invitation to go with them on their excursion, he had wandered about, looking at the different lions that came in his way, till, tired and dispirited, he began to think of returning home, when it occurred to him that he neither knew his way nor was he sufficiently accomplished to ask it.

From this dilemma the opportune appearance of his aunt's carriage extricated him, and he gladly availed himself of a seat in it, though he had an inward conviction he would be lectured about his wife's conduct the whole way home.

He did not know that since the misdemeanour of the morning, another cause of offence had come to light calculated to throw the former quite into shade, but of this he was not long left in ignorance, for Mrs. Bellingham opened fire without any unnecessary delay.

Of all things in the world to have come to her knowledge, this was precisely what Mark had most hoped and wished should *not*, and now she had the whole story at her fingers' ends !—

no—not quite the whole story, for it still remained for him to ascertain whether his precious
Theresa's little display of wilfulness, (as he
now so indulgently looked upon it) had been
discovered, or whether it were still in his power
to throw a cloak over it.

Of this his mind was soon satisfied, and then
he found courage to combat the point in a manner which he could not otherwise have done.

His imprudence, his folly, in not accompanying his wife wherever she appeared in
public was Mrs. Bellingham's chief grievance.
How could he allow that young creature to go
about by herself?—Was it idleness or heedless-
ness? what *was* it, in short? why did he not
follow her like a shadow? Surely, only married two months, it was not the trouble that he
grudged?

But Mark's conscience did not prick him
here;—he knew that from the hour they had
married, it had been his pride, his happiness,
his sole occupation to be by the side of her whom

he had chosen as his companion through life, and never once had he failed in this pleasurable duty save on this one unfortunate occasion— yet how could he explain to that severe judge that by no fault of his was this act of apparent negligence committed?—how could he tell her the facts of the case, or even if he found courage for that, how could he bear to sit and hear Theresa blamed?—impossible!—so he fought the battle artfully as well as manfully.

"You forget, my dear aunt, that on the evening in question, Theresa had the protection of her mother."

"Protection, indeed!—and you see where she took her! to the only house in the whole round of her circle to which she ought not to have gone!"

"Well," said Mark, raising his eyebrows, "it is all very well to insinuate so much against Mrs, Norman, but I only wish some one would have the goodness to tell me what it is they have to say against her;—can her faults take no shape? are they incapable of being embodied in language?"

How little did Mark Chetwode ever think he should be thus tempted, almost to stand up for the contemned Mrs. Norman!

"If they are," retorted Mrs. Bellingham, "it is because the world is less uncharitable towards her than towards most of its votaries; —I know nothing of her myself, beyond having heard that she is supposed to be a widow—but what I blame you for is, having sent your wife alone into the very heart of a set of people amongst whom you know as well as I do she had two or three serious admirers—you should be aware at your time of life, how much more prone men are to flirt with a young married woman than with a girl even, so"...

"I have no fears of Theresa, as far as conduct goes," interrupted Chetwode warmly, "and I am happy to say she has had no concealments from me; I was aware of Sir Henry Wharton's preference for her long ago, and aware also that she chose me when she might have had him instead, consequently of him I had no fears—neither did it occur to me that"...

He paused—for he then recollected the conversation he had had some few days before with Francis Keating, in which *two* of Theresa's conquests at Mrs. Norman's were named, but who was the second?

"Never mind what did occur and what did not occur to you—look sharper another time, that is all I have to say; as to Sir Henry Wharton he would flirt with a broomstick in petticoats—he flirts with Mary Vere there!—so he is not so dangerous, but young Sydenham was a much more serious affair, and a man of your age should know that"...

What a man of his age should know was lost upon Mark Chetwode, for that name, like a flash of light, had illumined all that had hitherto been dark to him, and he was plunged in the deepest of reveries long after his aunt had ceased speaking.

"Young Sydenham!" — what a chain of bygone days that name called back again—how well Chetwode remembered him!—how distinctly he recollected the first evening he had ever seen him, the night of the opera too, and the many succeeding evenings when, with his calm manners, his face of singular beauty, and his noiseless, unobtrusive presence he spent hour after hour in paying what Chetwode had till now actually thought were *impartial attentions* to the mother and her two young daughters !

Could it be possible that he had been deceived?—had it indeed been what Mrs. Bellingham called "a serious affair" between Sydenham and Theresa?—if so, then Chetwode's day-dream was over, and a future of anguish, silent and secret, was all he would have to look to!

Well, well, he now remembered his early pangs of jealousy, in those days when he first began to watch Theresa with interest, and to wonder if she had ever had a preference; well too did he remember his mother's declaration that had she herself been a young lady of eighteen, she should have required a lock and key for her heart, to guard it fromMr. Sydenham.

How heavily laden with bitterness did all these little trifling remarks and thoughts now come back to Mark Chetwode's memory, and had it not been for the presence of his aunt, he could have wrung his hands as they recurred, so fraught were they, to him, with grief and mortification.

Then again came another dreadful thought; —had Theresa, his own innocent Theresa, met this young Sydenham at Mrs. Norman's, and never mentioned it to him?—Could she, whose happiness he had so studied, prove so regardless of his own? or had she concealed the circumstance to avoid giving him pain, or causing him uneasiness ?

How ready he was to find any excuse for one so dearly, deeply loved!

Now too, he recollected Francis Keating's hesitation when speaking of the 'two' of Mrs. Norman's admirers, of whom Theresa had robbed her. Of course his brother-in-law knew that it had been a "serious affair," and hence arose his hesitation. Of course Edward Sydenham was the other of the 'two,' and possibly it was to prevent their meeting that Keating had placed the objectionable qualities of Mrs. Norman's house so strongly before him, not liking possibly to assign the real reason which ought to deter Chetwode from allowing his wife to enter that circle.

So reasoned he, on whom one of the worries of life was now falling for the first time; but it could hardly be called reasoning, for he was in so bewildered a state, that his thoughts were all mixed up together, and came rushing into his imagination, one over the other, without

form or order—he could think on no one point
at a time—all was confusion, and instead of
taking compassion on his state Mrs. Bellingham
only sat and eyed him with triumphant satisfaction, for she looked upon his mental suffer-
ings as merely repentance for the fault which
she had been kind enough to point out to him.

At last to his inexpressible relief, the carriage stopped at Meurice's, and he was let out
of his cage.

Descending with more alacrity than politeness he made his way instantly to his own
room, and there locking himself in, tried to
think coolly over all that had been said, and
resolve his mind as to what he should do.

To ask Theresa plainly, on her return,
whether she had met young Sydenham at Mrs.
Norman's that evening of the party was his
first idea, and then he retracted it, for it
struck him that it would be unwise to call up
the name unnecessarily, if indeed it had any
power still over Theresa, as his aunt had certainly insinuated;—his second thought was,

to ask Francis Keating, and from this too he shrank— he could not bear the idea of making any other person a party to the secret that was tearing his own heart; the secret of his unhappiness, and, perhaps groundless, jealousy; where then was he to apply? from whom was he to learn what he so anxiously desired to know, and that was, if Sydenham were now in Paris ; for in spite of all Mrs. Bellingham had said, his own open nature prevented his giving ready credence to stories of the duplicity of others, and he doubted—more than doubted—if Theresa had ever met him since their marriage; he ended by persuading himself that she never would have done so without mentioning it to him, and so he resolved to wait for a little while, and watch his opportunity. If anything should accidentally bring the name on the tapis, he would ask the question, but not unless—he *would* not doubt Theresa!

All this time he forgot Georgina—he forgot

that the question, simply asked of her, would be sure to to meet a straightforward answer, and all his anxiety would be set at rest; but people in a dilemma never will think of the right way of extricating themselves, and the matter-of-fact Mark Chetwode never saw anything that was not placed straight before him. As yet, the crooked ways of the world were unknown paths to him, and his honest, nnsuspicious. nature was likely to prove but a stumbling block in his road, for it blinded him to all kinds of guile.

Consequently, when Theresa came home from her drive, with her bright face, and her brilliant and amusing conversation, the past was all forgotten, and his melancholy ride with his aunt effaced from his memory. She was his own again, merry, happy, and full of enjoyment, and playfully asked him, even before she took off her bonnet, whether her not going the round of grand visits had mortally affronted " my aunt Bellingham ?"

Nevertheless during the calm hours that succeeded this troubled one, many and many a time did Mark Chetwode wish that by some means he could gain the information he required, and so have the satisfaction of telling Mrs. Bellingham that he had not been the imprudent husband that she had accused him of being; that in the first place Sydenham's preference was not for Theresa; in the next, that they had never met since her marriage.

Full of this subject, whilst Theresa was looking over some new books, he fell into one of the reveries which his quiet and solitary life had made habitual to him, and so often did he ask himself the question " where is he now?" that at last, almost without thinking, his thoughts turned into language, and he suddenly exclaimed—

" I wonder where Mr. Sydenham is now !"

At first Theresa did not answer; she was bending over her books, and continued doing so for some moments before she said—" Did you speak ?" and then he was obliged to repeat the sentence.

" He is *Captain* Sydenham now," was the reply.

" Is he?   What has become of him ?'

Theresa tossed back her ringlets, and walked towards the fire, by which her husband sat.

" I am sure I do not know,' said she, in a clear, unconstrained voice, " but I suppose in Ireland, where he was some months ago; what made you think of him ?"

" Merely a train of thought," said Mark, his heart beating quicker than usual with relief and pleasure, " and because he is associated in my mind with my first acquaintance with you. He was rather an admirer of yours, was he not, Theresa ?"

When people try to ask a question carelessly there is invariably some intonation of the voice which betrays them, and defeats their object ; Theresa distinguished that intonation in a moment, and smiled to herself, at the same time raising her eyebrows, and coquettishly screwing up her lips.

" Why, so people said! and perhaps it might have looked like it to those who did not know that we were brought up like brother and sisters; but for my part I used to think him very fond of Georgy."

" What took him to Ireland ?" continued Mark, still in the same indifferent voice.

" What would take men all over the world— money !" laughed Theresa; " some old aunt left him a fortune, I believe."

" Really? then why did he not come and marry Georgy ?"

Theresa hesitated; she began to suspect that Mark was growing deep—that he was *sounding* her in fact, and she felt herself getting warm; she looked full in his face, and as the uncertain flashes of the fire-light illumined it, she saw his eyes fixed steadily on her; this was Mrs. Bellingham's doing! this sudden curiosity about Edward Sydenham was some of *her* handiwork! and she forthwith set about acting her part better than her husband did his!

" Marry Georgy, my dear Mark? she would not have married *him!* that everlasting flute (of which I am so heartily sick that I wish I could do it an injury without being suspected,) made her deaf to every voice except Francis Keating's! poor Georgy! now I could *not* have married Francis, could *you?*"

" They seem very well suited; but you were going to tell me "—began Mark.

" Oh, yes; about Captain Sydenham's being my admirer; who said he was?"

Theresa was so abrupt sometimes, that her *brusquerie* had the effect of putting out her husband more than anything else. It disarranged all his ideas, and bewildered him; and on the present occasion he was rather confused as to how he should answer without giving up this authority, but luckily a happy reply came to his assistance.

" Why, I saw you together very often, did I not ?"

" I am sure you saw nothing of his admiring me *then*," retorted Theresa, exultingly; " no, no ; that will not do; somebody has been talking to you about it since *that !* come, confess ᴵ who said so ?"

Mark shook his head.

" But shaking your head is no satisfaction; was it Francis? did Francis say so? come, out with it; if he did I shall honor him with my company this evening."

" He did not, then," said Mark.

" Then who was it ?"

" My dear Theresa, I never told you that anybody said so !"

" Ah but I know somebody did!—look me in the face and deny it if you can !"—Mark laughed. " No you cannot: who was it then? —tell no stories about it, or else your mamma shall be informed of the bad tricks you have learnt in France. Was it Mrs. Bellingham ?"

"If I say it was, will you honour *her* with your company this evening? I assure you you could not gratify the old lady more than by going, uninvited, and offering to drink tea with her."

" Tell me first, was it Mrs. Bellingham?—now Mark, you know it was: oh, how could she be so silly. What did she say?"

Theresa's object was gained. She had turned the tables, and turned the cross-questioning; but she did not mean to turn the conversation till she had rendered whatever information Mrs. Bellingham had imparted, harmless.

To her husband's assurance that she said very little—so little that it only recalled Captain Sydenham to his recollection, Theresa proceeded,

"Did she say anything about mamma too? because we used to declare that when mamma found that neither of her daughters would take Edward Sydenham, she would marry him herself—that is, when she can find him, for she

was saying, only the other night, that this is
the first time in our lives that we have ever
been three months without knowing where he
is, exactly."

Chetwode breathed new life again; his
point too was gained, and his mind relieved of
its burthen. Now he could meet Mrs. Bellingham on equal ground; but still, little,
little indeed did he think, how dear a price he
had paid during the last few moments for the
knowledge he had so cautiously, as he thought,
drawn out.

He had opened Theresa's eyes to the fact,
that besides being acquainted with much of her
Parisian career, Mrs. Bellingham was now
making good use of the power it gave her, by
keeping up a system of *espionnage* which the
young wife was determined not to allow.

Her dislike to the old lady had begun at
Tunbridge-Wells, and she now saw that she
was dangerous as well as disagreeable; but
thanks to the simplicity of her husband's cha-

racter, she had learnt in time to be on her guard, and she would not rest till she had removed Mark from such objectionable influence —influence which had actually tempted him to lay aside his natural disposition, and beat about the bush for an answer to a question, which, if he had asked openly, she would have answered honestly.

At least she thought she would;—perhaps if it *had* been asked openly, she would have been offended, called him suspicious, distrustful, insulting, and made a scene.

Be that as it may, her inward satisfaction was very great, for a legitimate reason had been placed before her for hating Mrs. Bellingham, and she resolved that if ever Mark Chetwode took his aunt's part, and condemned her for her want of affection for her, she would inform him that her reasons for disliking that excellent relation were, that she had endeavoured to set the husband against his wife, by manufacturing stories behind her back.

G 5

Now it happened that as Mrs. Bellingham drove home, her conscience rather upbraided her for the warmth with which she had spoken to her nephew, and she began to have some misgivings as to whether she had been quite prudent in setting light to a train in his mind which never would have ignited of itself, for Mark was not naturally of a jealous temperament;—he had never yet had any cause for jealousy, for in the affections of those few on whom his own were placed, he had never had a rival, therefore, ·when she thought over all she had said, Mrs. Bellingham regretted having inflicted what must have been an acute pang to him, although she tried to repeat over and over to herself the antiquated motto—" I wound to heal."

" At all events," said she to Mary Vere in the course of her dialogue on the subject; " I am sorry I did not tell Mark that after all, perhaps, that young Sydenham is not in Paris. I was so engrossed with putting him on his guard, that it never occurred to me; my whole fear was, that his name should be disgraced by anything like a flirtation, particularly under the spiteful eyes of Mrs. Norman."

" But Mrs. Mark Chetwode was never much of a flirt, dear madam—was she?" said Mary Vere, in a kind of extenuating voice; and Mrs. Bellingham took her up so sharply that she quite started.

" How should you know, Mary Vere? How can one flirt judge of another? If you were not such an idiot, you would be the greatest flirt in existence yourself. But Theresa Dering was a *quiet* flirt—one of the most dangerous kind : it is just like children's games—when they make a noise, one knows they are all right, but the moment they are quiet, depend upon it they are in mischief. But Lord—bless —me—" and the old lady began rocking herself backwards and forwards, " why should I waste my breath;—why do I talk? The man is married, and the deed is done; but Mrs.

Dering's daughter is never the woman *I* should have chosen for my nephew's wife."

The companion sat mutely thinking over what had passed that day, and in her heart she longed for some stolen moment in which she could whisper to Mr. Chetwode what Mrs. Bellingham had just said, and thus, supposing he had been hurt by her lecture, heal the wound; she longed too to be able to say to him carelessly " Captain Sydenham is not even in Paris" for she had seen the expression of his countenance when the name was mentioned, and felt for him.

Yet how, was her second thought, could she do this without treachery to Mrs. Bellingham? for had she not, months before, allowed herself to be the vehicle by which Mark was to be warned of his impending danger, when first his attachment to Theresa Dering was suspected?

Certainly the case was now altered and Mark was " married and done for " as his aunt emphatically termed it, but still *her* position was thes ame—she was still dependent—still nothing but Mrs. Bellingham's companion, and she had no right to interfere.

From this inward cogitation she was roused by the cross voice of the old lady herself, directing her to take pen and ink and invite Mr. and Mrs. Mark Chetwode formally to dinner for the next day but one—Mrs. Bellingham did not consider them worth a longer notice, besides, what engagements could they have? who did they know in Paris to engage them, and if they projected going to any public place of amusement Mrs. Bellingham expected that that would be set aside.

" Now write another note," said she when the first was completed, " write, ' Mrs. Bellingham requests the favour' to Mr. and Mrs. Keating."

Mary Vere silently conplied and then looked up enquiringly—she could not help thinking that there was another note that ought to be written but she was afraid to prompt;—she

therefore looked the questions that she dared'
not ask.

" Old Mr. Cholmondeley—he called here
yesterday and to-day, all for a dinner I know;
ask him—and there are the D'Estervilles, good
people, and she is a pretty young woman; she
will play to Mrs. Keating's singing—now how
many is that ?"

" Just eight," said Mary Vere, for she knew
that she was never counted herself.

" Then do not ask the D'Esterville's for I
want you at table—I must have another man—
who *is* there?'

" Did you know," began the companion
timidly, " that Mrs. Dering is in Paris?—at
Meurice's? staying with Mrs. Mark Chetwode?"

" I know no such thing," retorted Mrs. Bellingham indignantly, " I am not supposed to
know of even the existence of Mrs. Dering!—
I have not the honour of being acquainted with

her, and I shall be obleeged to you not to dictate to me in matters of this kind—I told you I wanted a man."

Mary Vere drew a china bowl towards her and turned over the cards—

" Here is Lord Arthur Varley."

" A stupid young man—no—go on !"

" Sir Henry Wharton."

" One for me, and two for yourself!—no thank you! who else ?"

" Mr. Denis Rochfort."

" That will do !—don't confuse me by shuffling all those cards about—an Irishman and a Roman Catholic—but a gentleman all the same, and an excellent family ;—now begin, ' dear Mr. Rochfort.' "

" Yes ma'am —' my dear Mr. Rochfort——' "

" My dear ?—who said my dear, Mary Vere? are you out of your senses?—there is a vast difference between ' dear ' and ' my dear '— never let me find you putting in words of your own accord again—have you got to the end already ?—now then, address, and send them off directly, and at my nephew's let them wait for an answer, but no where else."

And the note found the Chetwodes at dinner.

CHAPTER VI.

BESIDE the Chetwodes that day at dinner sat Georgina, Mr. Keating, and Mrs. Dering, a merry family group, and Mark was laughing and talking over his wine glass full of walnuts, so delicately peeled by Theresa, as if his firmament had never known a cloud.

Mrs. Bellingham's servant, having been courteously received by Victor, began in the warmth of his heart, to divulge to that functionary that there was a dinner *en train,* and that he was also the bearer of other despatches, and amongst them, one to Mrs. Keating.

Victor then, as in duty bound, imparted to the man the secret of Mr. and Mrs. Keating's being actually in the hotel at that moment, and that by giving him the note it would save him a good walk; consequently the two notes went up together.

Georgina opened hers with the air of a person who does not know what to expect, then looked pleased and handed it to her husband with the words—

"How very civil, very kind too, of Mrs. Bellingham—we shall be very happy, shall we not?"

But upon Theresa's face a different expression sat.

First she looked at her mother—then round the table—then asked to see her sister's note, and then exclaimed,

"There must be some mistake!—*all* of us asked and Mamma left out?—Victor, is there not another?"

The effect of these words was wonderful—Mark Chetwode coloured to the very top of his forehead—Georgina bent over her plate till her face was not visible—Mr. Keating looked as if, in another moment, he should laugh, and Mrs. Dering kept making eyes and signs at Theresa as if to silence her.

And then Victor returned and said that there were no other notes—Mrs. Bellingham's servant had two more, but they were both to gentlemen.

" Very well," said Theresa hastily and imperatively, " then we will send an answer," and she flung the invitation over to her husband.

Mark read in silence, and whilst he did so, Theresa rose and walked towards a second fireplace that there was at the extremity of the room, followed by her mother, who, to do her justice, seemed more alarmed at her daughter's anger than at the slight put upon herself.

Georgy looked up at her husband. " I am

going to write a song," said he returning her glance.

" Really ?" was her answer, surprised at the strange announcement, " what has put that into your head—are you joking ?"

" No, 1 am only deliberating about the title —I don't know whether to call it " The Battle," or the " Breeze !"

And upon this Georgina laughed so heartily in spite of herself, that Mark Chetwode looked up in astonishment.

The changed and saddened expression of his countenance, however, checked her mirth, which was but momentary, and then came the question, who was going ?—Georgy and Mr. Keating meant to accept...it was so very attentive of Mrs. Bellingham—it would be so ungracious to refuse, for after all, she and Mrs. Dering had never met, except on the wedding morning, and then even, they had not been made acquainted with each other.

It went to Georgina's heart to see the almost grateful glance that Mark cast on her as she brought out in little disjointed phrases the above sentences, but Theresa answered vehemently,

"I call that no excuse at all!—their never happening to have been introduced is all nonsense!—as *my mother*, Mrs. Bellingham, should have included mamma, even if she had never known, until this moment, that there was a Mrs. Dering on the face of the earth."

"But my darling," began Mrs. Dering, in her smallest and most amiable voice, "I have been so remiss as never to have left a card on Mrs. Bellingham—you know I always made a point of doing so, and this time I am ashamed to say, what with your going out with Georgy to-day, and your own carriage being laid up, I have been completely prevented—the fault is all mine—I assure you it is!—Had I left a card, depend upon it my invitation would have accompanied yours."

"I do not believe it!" exclaimed Theresa, little thinking how near she was to the truth— "I believe it to be intentional neglect!"

Chetwode turned his head quietly towards her as she uttered these words, and fixed his calm, steady eyes on her face with a cold, half warning expression, that would have daunted many people, though it did not Theresa.

Oh!" thought Georgina, trembling for what might come next," "why does he sit so still!— —why does he not speak!—one effort, dear, good Mark, and you would be master for ever, yet you will not make it!"

"Mark," continued Theresa, after a pause, and seeing that no one seemed likely to speak, —"of course you do not expect me to accept this invitation?"

"My darling"...began Mrs. Dering again.

"Now, mamma, I entreat you not to interfere! if you have no regard for yourself, I have some for you; Mr. Chetwode must answer this note himself, and all I have to say is, that into a house from which my mother is excluded, *I will not go!*"

Georgina looked at Mark at that moment and she saw his lips quiver—no wonder!...and yet, how temperately he answered!—how mildly he apologised, in the first place, to Mrs. Dering, for the omission, mentioning at the same time his aunt's peculiarities, and her established rule never to have more than eight at her dinners, and when Mrs. Dering hastily and nervously accepted the reason as ample excuse, how gently he reminded his wife that this was probably a party made expressly for the brides, and that he advised her to copy Georgina's example, and take the civility as it was meant.

" Georgy may do as she likes," was Theresa's answer, "but I consider it an insult to mamma, and I will not go unless she is either included, or the omission explained."

" My darling," persisted poor Mrs. Dering, who in her heart was dreadfully afraid of Mrs.

Bellingham, and in agonies lest she should be drawn in to dining with her, " do you know as it happens, even had I been included, I doubt if I could have accepted, for to tell you a little secret, I am half engaged already for Thursday ; —indeed, my dearest, you must learn to control your filial affection a little more !"

Fortunate Mrs. Dering! to have hit upon so happy a phrase, when meaning to exemplify the passionate, and in reality, the vindictive, warmth of her daughter!

The fact was, that ever since Theresa had had that short *tête à tête* with her husband, in which the name of Captain Sydenham had been introduced, her feelings towards Mrs. Bellingham had undergone a considerable change for the worse, and the moment an opportunity occurred in which she could give vent to them in any shape, the torrent burst forth.

Of course the husband and family were ignorant of this exciting cause, and therefore it was, that the term " filial affection," was a pe-culiarly happy one, inasmuch as in the sight of Mark Chetwode, filial love was sufficient to·cover a multitude of sins.

The phrase acted like a charm upon him ; it mollified his suppressed anger, and poured balm upon his wounded feelings; it beautified the curling lip and the scornful eye of his " gentle Theresa," and brought a smile to his countenance as he said,

" Well—well; we will talk it over by and bye—there is no great hurry ; this little discus-sion must not spoil the harmony of our evening and stop up Keating's flute ; and you and I, Mrs. Dering, are going to have a game of piquet."

Theresa moved to the piano, and opened it, but before she let the subject drop, she could not resist saying, in spite of her sister's reproving glance—

" *You* may make a trifle of it, and pass it over lightly too if you please, but *I* shall not!"

As this was addressed to no one, no one replied; but as Georgina took her seat at the instrument, she shook her head and exclaimed,

" Oh, Theresa! value that man as he deserves! do not trifle with his temper in this way! see how kind and forgiving he is."

" Forgiving?" retorted Theresa, in the same low voice in which her sister had spoken—" it is for me to be forgiving I think! but never mind—never mind now—I will have my way in the end—mamma shall go there, I am determined—or at all events if she does not go, she shall be asked!" and so closed the evening.

When Theresa and her husband met at breakfast the next morning, Mark Chetwode had spent many long and wakeful hours in thinking over the events of the preceding day, and revolving in his mind what course he had best pursue so as to make all things smooth again.

That his aunt, unfortunately, was no admirer of his mother-in-law he knew perfectly well, and yet he could not help thinking that the present bold stroke was carrying hostilities rather too far, for it placed both himself and Theresa in an awkward position. If they declined this dinner, the offence would never be pardoned; if they accepted it, it was a tacit affront to his wife's mother, although certainly, as Mrs. Dering had said, Mrs. Bellingham was *not supposed to know* she was even in Paris, much less located in the very hotel with her daughter, and sitting at the same table when the unlucky notes arrived.

Oh, those convenient words "*not supposed to know!*" how safe a bulwark are they, behind which we may quietly shrink, when it suits our pleasure to make them act as an excuse for any little breach of courtesy which we think may " *tell* " upon the sensitive feelings of those against whom it may suit us to indulge some petty jealousy or private pique.

" Have you seen the A's yet?" Mrs. B

will ask of Mrs. C., who hates the A's, but dare not show it openly.

" No," will be Mrs. C's reply—" they have not called."

" But one of the daughters is dangerously ill."

" Really ?"

" Yes ; and they have been in Town this week or more."

" I know they have," returns Mrs. C. " but I am *not supposed to know that !*"

And yet the A's, in the midst of sorrow, sickness, and anxiety, must not complain of Mrs. C.'s neglect, because they have not called to let her know they are in town, although perfectly aware that she must have known the fact from Mrs. B.

And this is charity !—this the link of brotherly love and kindness which is *supposed* to connect the whole race of suffering human nature, one with another !

Mark Chetwode thought, that considering his aunt was now connected with Theresa and her·family by the ties of relationship through marriage, she might for once´ have waived acknowledged customs and old regulations, such as having four ladies and four gentlemen, and admitted Mrs, Dering to the circle.

He thought too that it was a pity that Theresa should not yield as graciously to the whims of a very old woman as had done both her sister and her mother, and then all would be smooth, but he began now to see into the character of his wife as clearly as he did into that of his aunt, and he tried in vain to decide in his own mind which would yield!

If both stood firm and refused to give up their point, then really the only alternative he saw, likely to be productive of peace, was, to vacate the field of battle at once, and leave Paris—after all, it would only be adhering to his original determination, and would excite but little surprise; and then he reflected with unfeigned regret that not eight and forty hours had his aunt been in Paris, yet she had already been the cause of two disputes—yes, disputes, for they were more than misunderstandings !—two disputes between himself and Theresa !

Better therefore that they should at once go ; and as the necessity presented itself, he sighed heavily and bitterly.

Attracted by the sigh, Theresa, who had till now sat opposite to him in silence, spoke.

" I can read your thoughts, Mark—you are thinking of this odious invitation ; now what are we to do ?"

" I wish I could answer the question," returned Chetwode, relapsing into his reverie ; and then it was Theresa's turn.

With the fluent vivacity which was her characteristic, she pointed out to him the slight that had been offered to her mother, and asked him what he would have felt had it been from *her* aunt towards *his* mother ? she asked him a thousand questions, and answered them all herself, and still her husband sat, his face buried in his hands, and uttered not a syllable.

" But what are we to do ?" he suddenly exclaimed; " how can we help it? you would not surely have me thrust Mrs. Dering upon the hospitality of my aunt against her will? your mother would resent that as a much greater indignity than the not being asked."

" I would have you do this," cried his wife ; " go to Mrs Bellingham—see her—say that on Friday we are to leave Paris, and that the fatigue of dining out on the eve of a journey must plead our excuse for declining her invitation !

" Leave Paris?" echoed Mark Chetwode to himself, as he gazed full of wonder at Theresa —could he have heard aright? or could he have been speaking aloud?—was it possible that she, who, a few hours before, had so violently opposed his wish to return to England, could now actually propose the measure of her own accord?—his delight was great, and he could hardly believe his ears or conceal his satisfaction, but the latter feat he *did* achieve, for experience had taught him wisdom, and a painful lesson it was, to learn to hide what would give him sincere pleasure, for fear it should meet with opposition from her who had sworn " to love, honour, and *obey* him! "

And now her enquiring eyes were on him, expecting an answer, and he hardly knew what to say!

" But suppose," he began, " suppose, Theresa, my aunt should refuse our apology?— Suppose she should *insist* on our going to her? —what am I to say in that case ?"

" Insist ?" Theresa smiled—" then you must get out of it as well as you can !—I can only say that unless Mamma either goes, or is invited, nothing shall induce me to enter the house, and I do not see how you could very well go without me, so perhaps the threatened loss of both of us may bring the old lady to her senses."

To hear his Aunt Bellingham spoken of in this way—she, to whom from his childhood he had always been accustomed to look up with respect bordering on awe, was something very new and strange to Mark Chetwode; but he was not in a frame of mind just then to take much notice of it—he felt low, nervous, and altogether unlike himself—well might Mrs. Bellingham say he was altered!—and taking his hat without uttering another word, he departed on his disagreeable errand, totally unfit to combat, yet fully aware that the errand was for that express purpose.

As soon as he was gone, Theresa went to her mother's room.

Mrs. Dering was breakfasting in bed according to her usual custom, and whilst in one hand was a large French roll, in the other was a small French novel;—she was not the least invalided, but morning dresses were expensive, so she always remained in bed (unless something unusual occurred to call her out of it,)

H 5

until two o'clock in the day, and then she
emerged, the airy, graceful, beautifully dressed
woman, after whose proceedings Victor considered it necessary to look with the eye of a
lynx.

This was her Parisian life; in Paris she was
not the humble, servile, and active mother—
the widow with the "small means" dependant
on the kindness of friends; no—here she was
in her natural atmosphere and element—making
a great show upon a very little, and not descending to anything derogatory—for, insinuating herself into an hotel as her son-in-law's
guest—dining upon every soul out of whom
she could coax or hint a dinner—and getting
presents of bonnets and dresses in a manner
totally incomprehensible to half the world,
she did not consider at all beneath her;—all
these things she looked upon as the natural
consequences of being a widow,—therefore
when Theresa had talked to her for about an
hour, and made her comprehend that the object

of her visit was to extort from her a promise that if Mrs. Bellingham's invitation should arrive, she would decline it, Mrs. Dering did not know whether to be relieved or chagrined.

Fear had wrung from her the preceding evening the faintly-breathed announcement that she thought she was already more than half-engaged for the evening in question, but now a vague idea, that it was a good thing to be seen at Mrs. Bellingham's select table, and to be numbered amongst her distinguished few, made her regret that announcement, so she was rather annoyed with Theresa, and began arguing the point with the peevish impatience of a child.

But Theresa was firm. — She was determined that Mrs. Bellingham should not have the triumph of thinking that after coolly insulting *her mother* one day, she had only to hold up her finger the next, and beckon her to her table.

Passionate and ill-regulated as Theresa was, she was, on these points, more high-minded

than the wily widow; and now that Mrs.
Dering had no great object to gain by pushing
into good society, that young daughter would
not suffer her to stoop to attain a single step
through the aid of Mrs. Bellingham, and
hence arose her interdict.

At last Mrs. Dering was induced to promise;
—she thought it rather ridiculous, rather hard
too, but promise she did, and then Theresa
told her of their probable departure on Friday,
asking her at the same time what she meant
to do?—had she seen anything likely to suit her
in the course of her wanderings? or did she
mean to stay at Meurice's until she had found
her *pied à terre?*

The sudden shock of this " warning to
quit" startled Mrs. Dering almost out of her
senses, and in the few moments which she took
to collect her ideas, she had been metaphorically
scampering round to all the shops where she
had lately been making a great show, and
tremblingly counting up the hundreds of francs

she owed at each, for though she never bought any expensive article, her purchases now and then were very numerous and " mounted up" as all small bills do, in a most unaccountable manner;—so much so, that whenever Mrs. Dering changed her lodgings or left town, a battle royal took place between herself and her tradespeople, consequent upon a known delusion of hers, that she was cheated by everybody.

Hitherto Victor had been her champion ; it remains to be seen whether he continued so after her acquisition of two sons-in-law.

After this momentary ramble Mrs. Dering's thoughts reverted to Theresa's last question, and she confessed that as yet she had found no domicile—that really she had been so occupied that she had not had time to look much about, but that she would see about it that very day, with Victor if he could be spared—and then Theresa left the room.

Victor was now summoned to a conference, and his customary " *Bien, madame*," was uttered in so hesitating a voice that Mrs. Dering saw he had something to suggest, and begged him to speak, if it were so.

Yes; he certainly had something to say, though he could not take the liberty to suggest, but had Madame forgotten that Monsieur Chetwode had taken his apartments at Meurice's *by the month?* and that full three weeks of the third month still remained? why did not Madame continue in them that time? Monsieur Chetwode could never object to this arrangement, since he would have to pay, even if the apartments were not occupied—why then need Madame hurry?

" But Victor, even supposing that to be the case, the *actual living* would be far beyond my small means! breakfasts and dinners, and all that—"

" But madame," exclaimed the ' treasure of

a man,' " all that is included! Monsieur Chetwode placed the arrangements in my hands and this was the plan agreed on !"

Mrs. Dering was silent, but her heart beat fast with delight. What an opening! what an opportunity ! it might never occur again ; and if she could only speak to Theresa before Mr. Chetwode's return, all might be managed, so ringing the bell impetuously for her old maid, she cast aside her French roll and her French novel, and prepared to rise.

She was in time ; her son-in-law had not returned, and boldly dashing at once into her subject, she told Theresa that having thought over her plans, she thought, by dint of great good management, she might be able to take the apartments, now in their occupation, *off Mr. Chetwode's hands* for three weeks, since that was the extent of the term for which they were engaged.

" And Victor tells me my dearest, that

there will be no reduction in their price, even though they stand empty all that time."

Theresa's cheeks burned like fire as her quick eye saw her mother's drift, and she felt so repugnant to the mean object at which she was so evidently aiming, that she pretended to take her at her word, and carelessly twisting her ringlets round and round her fingers without looking up, said she would mention the offer to her husband, for that she had no idea on what terms their suite had been engaged.

Mrs. Dering, however, was as sharp as her daughter, and soon espied the spirit in which her plan had been received; she saw that her fate hung on a thread, and she preferred trusting it to Mark than to Theresa, now that she saw the humour she was in; she therefore volunteered to speak to him as soon as he came home, but this was immediately negatived. Theresa liked to rule, order, and if necessary, blindfold her husband herself, but she gave up the power to no one else, "and so," said she, rising to put an end to the conversation, "I will mention it to him myself this evening—if I think of it—and I dare say he will be very much obliged to you."

And now to follow Mark Chetwode on his disagreeable mission.

The nearer he approached his aunt's house, the more uncomfortable he felt at the errand he was on; he wished, heartily, that he had thought of asking Georgy to let him be the bearer of her note of acceptation, for that might have smoothed the way for the unpleasant task of fishing for an invitation for an unwelcome guest, and made his opening speech easier; as it was, he had nothing to say but the very truth in all its ugliness; and as he was ushered into Mrs. Bellingham's presence, the aspect of affairs was anything but inviting.

The old lady was sitting close to the fire, buried in an old-fashioned arm-chair, and knitting a rug with the coarsest yarn and the

largest pins that were ever seen. From childhood Mark had seen that very piece of work in
her hands, and it seemed as if it neither waxed
larger, nor diminished, for it was only a "show"
piece, and he knew very well that its appearance was always the signal of a storm brewing.

By her side sat Mary Vere, and a book—
the book too was for show, as Mrs. Bellingham's eye-sight did not permit of her knitting
more than six stitches without dropping one,
and it was her custom to say whenever this
occurred, not that her powers of vision were
failing, but that she had not been attending, so
then the book was laid down, the stitch picked
up, and the farce began again.

When Mark entered, his aunt said nothing,
but she did much worse, for she fixed her eye
on him with a look which said more than many
words, and which mentally uttered in most
expressive language the sentence—"So you
have condescended to come with an answer at
last ?"

It often happens, however, that where gentleness will disarm and soften to repentance, a harsh word or look makes the offender stand up for himself and exhibit a spirit which would otherwise have lain dormant.

So it was with Mark Chetwode. His aunt's reception was so chilling, her first words too were so angry, that, although Mark knew she had some cause to lecture him for keeping her so long without an answer,—a negligence that no one easily forgives when a dinner party is in question—he did not think she had any right to cut so very severely though indirectly, at Theresa, and he put her down rather hastily.

" The fault was not my wife's—it was mine," said he, though his conscience gave him a twinge as he spoke. " No answer to your kind invitation could be given until I ascertained whether you were aware that Mrs. Dering was staying with us?"

" Staying with you?" echoed the old lady— "staying with you, or staying in your hotel?—

which?—if the former, how came you not to tell me?"

"Staying in our hotel," answered Mark, "but sitting at our table when your note arrived."

"And do you expect me to ask to my table every soul who happens to be sitting at yours when my invitations are being issued?" retorted Mrs. Bellingham.

"Certainly not, but considering that the lady in question is Theresa's mother, we certainly did think that you were not perhaps aware of her being in Paris, and therefore that the omission of her name in our invitation was accidental on your part...an oversight in short."

Mrs. Bellingham drew in her lips, and leaning back in her chair gazed intently at the fire for some moments, and then, across the wizened old face there gleamed a smile from which Mark turned away his eyes, so full of malicious pleasure and contemptuous laughter did it seem.

" Humph !" she ejaculated after the reverie was over, " so that is what you have come about, eh ?—is it ? to get me to ask Mrs. Dering to my party ?—very well—to invite a lady with whom I have not the honour of being acquainted— *your wife's mother !*"—and the old lady suddenly raised herself and turned towards her nephew with her dim old eyes quite lighted up—" that is your errand is it ?"

At that moment Mark Chetwode felt heartily ashamed !—ashamed of his mission and ashamed of himself, but luckily his aunt left him no time to stammer out an improved version of the story.

" Very well ! Mrs. Dering's daughter has married my nephew and my nephew requires that I should consider that he has married the whole family !— with all my heart;—but the character of my party is now changed, so sit down Mary Vere, and make my number twelve at once ;—ask the D'Estervilles, and Sir Henry Wharton, and be very particular not to forget

Mrs. Dering—but I forgot—of course Mark
Chetwode, you mean to be the bearer of *that*
yourself!"

It was very evident that Mrs. Bellingham
was seriously annoyed;—it was plain that
respect for the name of Chetwode alone, made
her give way on a point on which she had
never hitherto given up one inch of her ground,
namely, the guests of her dinner table, and as
Mark stood at the window, vacantly watching
the snow-flakes as they floated by, he wished
secretly that he had never been persuaded to
undertake the mission at all, for what had he
gained by it to compensate him for the anger
and contempt of the irate old lady, who had so
haughtily and so satirically conceded to his request.

The worst of it was that he felt it had not
been an open, striaghtforward, request!—he
had hinted, he had beat about the bush, he
had descended to ' fishing ' for an invitation—
he had lowered himself in his own eyes in fact,

and unquestionably so in the eyes of his aunt!

The feigned politeness, also, with which she had complied was very galling to him; it was so unlike Mrs. Bellingham to be polite!—in short he had hardly patience to wait for the note, and still less to frame some sentence expressive of his obligation, so anxious was he to be out of the oppressive atmosphere of the house, and breathing the fresh air of the streets, albeit in the midst of a snow-storm.

At last Mary Vere had accomplished her task, and the note was in his pocket.

" I wish you good morning," said his aunt, vehemently stirring the fire when he advanced to shake hands, and thus evading the ceremony, " I wish you good morning, and I am only sorry that my table does not admit of my including amongst my guests, your friend, Mrs. Norman!"

* * * * * * *

" Theresa! Theresa!" thought Mark to himself as he walked home, " all this is for your sake, otherwise it would be very hard to bear!" and he entered the hotel with a step as heavy as though all the cares of the world were already on his shoulders, and his heart was heavy also.

CHAPTER VII.

THERESA was waiting and watching for him at the window when he made his appearance, but she scanned his countenance with a scrutinizing glance before she spoke, and by that time he had advanced to the fire, shaken the snow flakes from his coat sleeves, and throwing the note on the table, abruptly exclaimed—

" There it is!—there is the note—but remember, Theresa—never send me on such an errand again."

VOL. II

She read it in silence—then turned and looked at the address, and calmly refolding it said—

" Well! I am glad the invitation is given—*l'amende* is made; but as it happens, mamma cannot accept it."

Mark repeated her words in unbounded surprise; not accept an invitation extorted with such difficulty?—decline going, after having almost, in plain words, asked for it?—surely Theresa must be joking!

" Indeed I am not. Mamma is engaged—you need not look so angry, just as if it were my fault—I cannot help her being engaged."

" Since when have you known it?—since when was this engagement contracted?" asked her husband, the calm current of his blood beginning to grow warm, though not absolutely to boil.

" I have known it since you went out; as for the date, you must have heard mamma say at dinner yesterday that she was more than half engaged for to-morrow, and as of course she could not know of your application to Mrs. Bellingham, she is now *quite* engaged—irrevocably—only I was determined she should be invited!''

Was this Mark Chetwode's reward! were these unkind, these unworthy sentences all his thanks for undertaking a most unpleasant mission, and placing himself in a most unenviable light in the opinion of his aunt!

He was bitterly vexed!—he tried in vain to conceal it, and as he paced the room and by preserving a strict silence, endeavoured to hide his displeasure and annoyance, a vague question, quenched though, almost as soon as embodied, arose in his mind,—was this the unalloyed happiness of married life?—was this the unity of thought, word, wish, and will?—was this the sympathy of souls, the one heart and the one mind?

Alas! alas!—had Mark Chetwode suffered those questions to dwell for one instant on his

imagination, another, a final one, might have
sprung up, more painful still to answer, and he
might in very bitterness have asked himself—
" Am I happy? am I even as happy as I was?"

The entrance of Mrs. Dering just then
was well-timed—it broke the uncomfortable
silence of the husband and wife, and as Mr.
Chetwode placed his aunt's note in her hands,
he earnestly requested her if possible to oblige
him by accepting the invitation it conveyed.

Poor Mrs. Dering was sadly, sorely, perplexed! Mark had always shown her so much
kindness, so much consideration—he had always been so deferential in his manner, and so
generous in his conduct towards her, that when
he so impressively requested her to accept his
aunt's invitation, her usual tact utterly failed
her, and so divided was she between the fear of
offending him and the fear of Theresa's firm eye,
just then fixed on her with unflinching steadi-
ness and volumes of meaning, that she coloured,
hesitated, stammered, and broke down in the

midst of the high flown expressions of thanks and apologies which she tried in vain to articulate!

Now all this was incomprehensible to her son-in-law ; he looked from one to the other, utterly unable to comprehend the conduct of either, but at last, half pitying the confusion of Mrs. Dering, he helped her by some timely phrases, common-place enough, but still tending to restore her equanimity.

He asked if her engagement were indeed one which she could not set aside, and learning that it was, partly by her own confession and partly by the words thrown in here and there in Theresa's imperative voice, he felt that there was nothing left but to make the best of it, and so convinced was he that Mrs. Bellingham's anger would be, by this final stroke, raised to its crowning pitch, that he purposed immediately going back and explaining it to her.

To this, however, his wife would not consent.

" How can you possibly wish to trouble yourself so exceedingly in a matter in which, after
all, neither you nor 1 are in any way concerned!
it is snowing heavily, and you are already so
damp that I feel quite chilly whenever you
come near me ; what is the use of traversing
these wretched streets again on such a day !"

" To prevent any uncomfortable feeling on
the mind of my aunt, and to carry Mrs. Dering's apology," answered Chetwode.

" As to the latter, Victor is the most proper
messenger, and as to the former, I really do
not see what it signifies, even supposing your
aunt should be desperately offended, for Mrs.
Bellingham appears to consider my mother
and her set, so immeasureably beneath herself
and hers, that there can be little fear of their
encountering each other after we are gone !
and that reminds me, are we to go on Friday,
or wait till Monday or Tuesday ?"

Mark was not sorry that a speech which had
jarred on every nerve in his body should be

wound up by a question which prevented the
necessity of his taking notice of what had preceded it; so, from pure dread of any further
cause for altercations which made him miserable,
he told Theresa that any day she liked would
suit him, only begging that it might not be a
later one than she absolutely wished.

`The following Monday was therefore fixed
on, and Mrs Dering, who during the last few
minutes had been standing in a distant window,
pretending neither to see nor hear, now
emerged from her hiding-place, and gave
Theresa a significant glance;—she thought it a
good opportunity for introducing the subject of
her future stay at Meurice's, and she also
thought that if she could possibly be in the
room when her liberal proposal was made to
Mr. Chetwode, it might be all the better for
her, as she was very certain from the specimen
of Theresa's management of her husband, to
which she had just been witness, that what-

ever plan the wilful young lady had in her head, she would carry it.

Theresa however took no notice of the glance; she turned from it indeed, and though Mrs. Dering recollected that she had said she would speak to Mark "in the evening," she also recollected that she added the doubtful clause "if I think of it,"—therefore though frightened to death lest she should be privately reprimanded for her audacity, she took courage to speak, not addressing herself particularly to either her daughter or her son-in-law, but indirectly suiting her sentences to either, or both.

A review of the events of this morning will have shown how much the spirits of Chetwode had been tried and harassed, leaving him in fact at the termination of the discussion, so depressed, and so worn out, that for 'peace and a quiet life' he would have agreed to almost any proposition in the world; he had been much distressed too, at the presence of Mrs. Dering during Theresa's speeches, and felt far more for her than she did for herself, consequently, when she made the object of her flowery discourse intelligible to him, his instant thought was, how he could best convey to her his wish that she should occupy the apartments after the departure of himself and Theresa, considering herself as his guest.

He felt an awkwardness in doing this, because he knew that poor people are generally very sensitive on the score of their poverty, and he was really anxious to word his kindness so as not to wound her feelings.

Mark Chetwode little knew what Mrs. Dering's feelings were made of! he only knew that her circumstances were not prosperous— he well knew the sound of her favorite expression "small means," two words which she used to every friend and acquaintance she had, at least three hundred and sixty five times in the course of the year ; but he did not know that there was little occasion for so much delicacy in making the arrangement, and that all his trouble to frame it in proper language was thrown away.

Mrs. Dering's delight was very great; her obligation unbounded, and Mark, with awkward vivacity, silenced the thanks which she poured forth;—at first she would not hear of it—she could not possibly accept—because she entreated dear Mr. Chetwode to recollect that she had already been nearly a fortnight in the hotel—suppose he permitted her to consider herself his visiter during *that* time, but not henceforth?

" During that time, this time, and time to come!" said he, in a cheerful tone of decision, a smile at the moment coming over his face like the gleam of a watery sun; " suffer me, my dear Mrs. Dering, to take all these mundane matters off your hands;—*lone ladies* have no business with hotel bills, so pray say no more about it."

And so it was settled; and Mark Chetwode, damp, cold, and uncomfortable, yet inwardly pleased at having been the source of such apparent pleasure and happiness to at least one person that day, retired to his room to shut himself in, and ostensibly to change the wet garments in which his wife had allowed him to hold so protracted a conference.

In the welcome quiet and silence of that room, somehow or other his thoughts wandered back to the first day of Mrs. Dering's arrival, and to Mr. Keating's prophetic remark on the occasion, as to her intention of becoming her son-in-law's guest.

"Do not think you will escape the honour she has destined you," had been his words, and certainly they had come true, and yet it never struck Chetwode that there had been any pre-concerted plan, or even hope—he would as soon have thought of suspecting Mrs. Dering of picking his pocket—in fact when that remark recurred to him, his predominant feeling was, satisfaction at having been able thus accidentally to heal the wound which the intentional slight, offered her by his aunt the preceding day, must have occasioned.

It has been said that Theresa was vain—but everything that she put on generally became her, and it was so easy for her to look well that she never considered twice what she was to wear, whilst with Georgy, the dress for the evening was an important subject which sometimes engrossed her attention for days before the occasion arrived.

That evening she looked in for a moment alone, to see what dress Theresa was going to wear, and when it was decided, she casually remarked,

" I wonder who we shall meet ?"

Theresa had no idea, but Mark who was sitting over the fire with his newspaper, looked up and said,

" I know; at least I know who is asked—an old friend of my aunt's, Mr. Cholmondeley—a Mr. Rochfort, Sir Henry Wharton and a Monsieur and Madame D'Esterville—"

" The D'Estervilles !" exclaimed Georgina. " Oh, Theresa ! *that horrid girl !*"

That was all she said, but her countenance was so expressive that when she was gone, Mark could not resist asking why Georgy had indulged in language so unusually strong for her.

" Thereby hangs a tale," said Theresa, " and I will tell you as a secret; Madame D'Esterville is an Englishwoman, and we three were all girls together; we had all the same admirers, I believe, only Annie D'Esterville was said to be desperately in love with Mr. Keating—some say he did not behave well—all I know is, she used to flirt with him till every one was scandalised, and at heart, Francis Keating is a finished flirt ;—however Georgy won him from her, and she married old D'Esterville directly —out of spite, no doubt, but still Georgy never could bear her, and I daresay she is rather annoyed now to think that Francis will be thrown in her way again."

"I should think Georgy could have little cause for fear," remarked Chetwode, "I never saw a better matched pair than she and her husband, and he seems devoted to her."

"He has never been tried yet," said Theresa coolly, and Mark, in his simplicity, wondered within himself when that young girl could have found time to have learnt so perfectly the many artful ways of the world we live in!

At last the hour for Mrs. Bellingham's dinner party approached, and Theresa stood dressed in her most elegant costume, awaiting the appearance of her husband.

At that time the Norma wreaths had just come in, and Theresa wore a green one; she looked like a Sappho, for her hair was put back to suit the style of head dress, and when Mark looked at her, he wondered to himself whether it were possible to see a being more beautiful.

Theresa's beauty was that of a statue— there was no fault of feature, no fault of figure;

the former were small and regular, and the latter moulded so perfectly that in whatever position she stood, it looked to advantage. She was not very tall, neither was she slight; considering her age she was on a large scale— but it was the *tout ensemble* that was so worthy of admiration, and her eyes and eyelashes were the great charm of her face, those deep, grey, velvet eyes, were so brilliant, so speaking, and so beautifully sly !

It has not been said that Theresa's face was faultless—on the contrary, it was remarkable for a want of expression; the little expression there was, was unpleasing, and to strangers there was an angularity which gave room for people to have divers opinions as to its perfection.

Her voice too was particularly disagreeable; sharp, high-pitched, and rapid in articulation— so that to be considered faultlessly lovely, Theresa Chetwode should have sat still, without uttering a syllable or more than half raising her eyes.

Nevertheless, on entering Mrs. Bellingham's rooms the next evening, the old lady was struck; she had seen but little of her before; once they had met at Tunbridge Wells, and Theresa was then looking ill; the next time she was a bride, and brides all look so much alike, if clad in the conventional dress, that Mrs. Bellingham had merely acquiesced in the general remark which she had heard uttered at every wedding she had ever attended,

" What a pretty bride she makes;" just as if a bride were a character and an apparition composed by the united care of a dress-maker and a hair-dresser, with a regular part to play for a few hours, played by all alike, but which all learn by intuition.

The old lady was very much pleased and satisfied with her appearance;—she received her quite courteously, and Mark did not know whether to attribute her graciousness to admiration, or to an excuse which had just arrived from Sir Henry Wharton, making her table even, when she thought Mrs. Dering's absence had made it odd.

Mrs. Bellingham sat in great state that day; she had on a new black velvet dress, and as it was trimmed all down the front in the most miraculous manner with bugles, which were just introduced, it was conjectured to be worn for the first time.

She had on a cap too, which had the credit of being *de la dernière mode,* yet somehow it bore the look of the ark, and the days of the deluge about it, most likely from its having undergone a little improvement at her own hands before she considered it fit to be worn.

On her hands were a pair of white kid gloves, which literally hung in bags about her fingers, and by her side, in exquisite contrast to the polyglot figure she presented, depended a costly *châtelaine.*

One curl of her light and juvenile wig was brought down over the eye that would not bear looking into, and the rest of them each went their own way, some turning one way and some the other, till the whole was wonderful to behold, and this was the wig which she assured everyone was a fac-simile of her own hair at the age of seventeen.

Mr. Cholmondeley was the only person who dared shake his head when this assertion was made.

Theresa had made up her mind that Mrs. Bellingham should not, as on former occasions, draw Mark to her side that evening, and monopolize his attention, instilling perhaps into him, dangerous or objectionable information; she therefore kept close to him, and made him play at various games, with which the tables were covered.

Mrs. Bellingham did not approve of this conduct at all, and made a memorandum in her own mind that the first moment she had an opportunity of speaking to Mark, she would tell him what an unpardonable breach of good taste it was in new married people, to make themselves conspicuous in society—but this opportunity Theresa effectually prevented;—her husband was like a bird under the fascination of a snake; too happy to bask in her smiles, and sun himself in her good-temper, he neither wished, nor was he able, to break the charm, but remained by her side, immoveable.

Georgina and Mr. Keating on the contrary never went near each other except once during the evening, and that was to sing a duet.

Perhaps there were two reasons for this;— one was, that they had made a rule from the beginning never to do so; the other, that when Mr. Keating's delighted eyes caught sight of Madame D'Esterville that evening, he could not leave her an instant.

It was years, (so he said, though it was only months) since they had met, and both had

married in the interim, consequently they had
a great deal to converse about.

Georgina's placid temper was all but ruffled
at his conduct; she thought it so very foolish,
considering that this was his first appearance
before Mrs. Bellingham as a married man, and
knowing that he had the reputation of a flirt,
it quite vexed her to think he was putting it in
Madame D'Esterville's power to tell everyone
he was " an old flirt of hers."

Young married women like their husbands
to " take up a position," as the saying is, and
not descend to the frolicsome manners of their
bachelorhood, and Georgina was very anxious
that Mrs. Bellingham should like Mr. Keating
and herself.

For herself she need not have feared. She
won the old lady's heart in that one short evening, for, once seated at the piano, it was difficult for any who heard her, to allow her easily
to leave it again, and she went on, singing song

after song, till Mrs. Bellingham, out of charity, allowed her to approach the fire and join the circle round it.

She was delighted with her unaffected grace and good humour—Georgina's greatest charm in Mrs. Bellingham's eyes was, the little likeness she bore to her mother, whilst Theresa was Mrs. Dering's counterpart!

Before the evening finally closed, however, the hostess determined to speak to her nephew, and sending Mary Vere on the errand, she desired him to come to a seat by her armchair.

He did so, but at the same time Theresa took a chair near enough to hear all that was said.

" So!" began Mrs. Bellingham in a stage whisper, " you are going to-morrow, are you?"

Mark answered that they had postponed their departure until the following Monday.

" And you winter in London?"

" Yes."

" Living with your mother, eh?"

" Yes—it has always been my mother's wish."

" Ha !" ejaculated Mrs. Bellingham, " she does not know yet...wait till you have tried it ...it won't answer—mark my words if it does !"

" I see nothing against it," returned Mark, " Theresa is such a favorite of my mother's— the house in Hill street is a good size, and altogether, we look upon it as our home without any misgivings."

" It won't answer," repeated Mrs. Bellingham, " take my word for it !—I do not give you my advice, because people never take advice ; human nature itself prompts one to rebel against advice, in fact to go directly in opposition to it, so if I had said to you, ' go and live with your mother in Hill-street,' I should have expected you to have gone and taken an unfurnished house in Lowndes-square, where you may have a choice ! however—it is nothing to me—tell me only, what are you going to do with that fine Frenchman? is he yours, or Mrs. Dering's?"

At this moment Theresa looked up quietly from the book of engravings she was examining, and smiling most unconsciously at her husband said—

" Is Mrs. Bellingham speaking of our Victor?—oh, dear madam, he is ours, not mamma's, now, I am glad to say, for I do not know what dear Mark would do without him!—he is quite invaluable to us, and we could not spare him, even to mamma!"

Mrs. Bellingham looked at her nephew, but he gave no answering glance, for his eyes were intently fixed on the fire;—she then looked at Theresa, but the pretty vacant stare gave back no satisfactory intelligence.

" He is hen-peeked!" said the old lady to herself—" he dare not say his soul is his own— the man is hen-pecked!—and so I said he *would* be!"

And thus finished that evening, and everyone,

almost, went to their homes dissatisfied, as is often the case, after a party on which we have built great hopes.

Mark thought Theresa had not made a favourable impression; Theresa thought Mrs. Bellingham would have a struggle before she relinquished all power over her nephew; Georgina was sick at heart, for, perhaps unintentionally, her husband had deeply vexed her by his silly flirtation with Madame D'Esterville, and this was her first vexation since her marriage, and Mr. Keating, before closing his eyes for the night could not resist saying—

"Georgina, my dear, that fellow, D'Esterville, is a great fool. What could make that girl take him?"

"How should I know, Francis?"

"Perhaps she was hard-up, eh?"

"I am sure I cannot tell."

"Well, but you know she would have had *me* any day."

"Then she must have been '*hard-up*,'" said

Georgy, trying to laugh; "but as she took him in preference, the compliment is questionable. If I were a man, I should not like to be the forlorn hope."

And so closed the last day of the year.

It may be naturally supposed, without any unnecessary romance, that the recurrence of the first day of a new year must bring with it, to every mind, a varied train of thoughts and images—some happy and some sad, yet all serious, for it is serious to look forward upon nothing but uncertainty, and equally so to look back upon the past, whatever it may have been, for it is gone for ever and ever to us, upon earth.

Even the young and light-hearted *wonder* what the new year will bring forth; but the old do not wonder, they rather wait, and breathe inward hopes, troubled by fears, for no new years' eve ever yet arrived, untinctured with this kind of sadness to them—perhaps to all.

Who can expect or hope that through the

long time of months, weeks, days, and hours, comprised in the one short word, we can escape free from all sorrow, all sickness and all adversity — and it is this that makes a New Year's Eve more one of trembling and foreboding, than of unalloyed anticipations.

Had Mark Chetwode married on a New Year's Eve, his gaze on the future might have been one of dazzled happiness, for no man ever entered on the new life with more joy and hope; but a drop of bitterness had mingled with the cup of sweets since his wedding-day, and he sat alone that last night of the year, full of thought, full of anxiety; lost in conjectures yet earnestly praying within himself that all might turn out for the best, and that he and one dearer than himself might still be as happy as they had hoped to be.

Meanwhile, Theresa was asleep, soundly and peacefully, and dreaming, most likely, of all the presents she was sure to receive the next day, and when that day dawned she had no reason to be disappointed, for of every size and shape the pretty trifles poured in.

Mark, whose costly taste rejected the mass of *bon-bons* which others sent to his young wife, placed on her table a gift of great value, and was annoyed to see that a box on which was written "*Papeterie*," but which contained sweets made to imitate everything for the writing table, divided her attention and admiration with his magnificent casket of old Dresden.

But the merry day closed without a cloud, and so it was a happy one to him, and then began the active preparations for departure.

It was in a moment of confusion such as attends all families on the move, that the talents of Victor shone conspicuous, and in the present case his master had literally no trouble, for he saw no packing going on, heard no noise, had no bills to look over, no arrangements to make, —but all was done, as if by some unseen agent, and Mark, who like all who have lived a life of luxurious ease, detested trouble, acknowledged of his own accord to Theresa that the man was an excellent servant—and in short, invaluable.

"I told you so," was Theresa's answer; "only you were very much inclined to disbelieve me: another time I hope you will not be so illiberal as to condemn a servant, because he happens to be a foreigner."

Mark knew that he had never been guilty of that crime; he knew that it was not he who had shrank from retaining Victor (and so did Theresa). He felt that that was a weakness on the part of his mother, which he hoped to conquer when he told her of the many excellent and efficient qualities which the man possessed, to counterbalance his only fault. But this he kept to himself, for till then his mother and her every thought, word and action, had been all-perfect in his estimation, and he could not bear that, even by inference, the slightest shadow of blame should ever attach to her whose foibles even, were sacred in his eyes.

In the midst, however, of the pleasant sort
of excitement of the last few hours, a circumstance occurred which tended more, perhaps,
to put Theresa on her best behaviour than anything which her husband could possibly have
devised.

Though her *trousseau* had been a very fair,
and considering her mother's "*small means*," a
very ample one; still there were omissions
in it which a few months of prosperity had
taught Theresa she could not possibly do without.

She had not, in the first place, a *cachemire*
of any kind—and how could a married woman
do without one? She had, therefore, chosen a
beautiful white shawl, and when she wore it,
her husband remarked that it looked cold, so
she bought a red one.

Then she had not a velvet dress when she
married, so a black one was ordered immediately,
and Mark, on her first appearance in it—unaccustomed to ladies' attire—fancied she was

in mourning, and thought it looked funereal; and having an idea that a velvet dress was no inconsiderable pull upon a purse, begged her to select one of a less sober hue, as his present.

Then she had no furs, and they too were procured. In short, there was no end to the positively indispensible articles of attire which, one after another, mounted up into a sum of some three or four thousand francs, a total which so terrified the young girl who had been accustomed to look upon an outlay of a hundred francs as an extravagance which could hardly ever be atoned for, that she crushed the bills in her hands, hid her face in the sofa pillows, and sobbed like a child.

The grief and dismay of Mark Chetwode on finding her in this state could not be described, and his delighted surprise on discovering the real cause, was a relief to his wife which at first she could hardly realize.

That he should think so little of money as to laugh so heartily when, one after the other, she told him the total of each bill, absolutely amazed her, but she was still more amazed when, after having . stammered forth a hope that future economy would enable her very soon to refund the allowance which she fancied he was advancing for her, he unhesitatingly said, no; that their visit to Paris had been a frolic, and he wished her to leave it without a single unpleasant reminiscence.

Theresa had bought that, he should hardly

trary, he was happy that she had procured all she required, and begged her to consider and remember that the allowance he had placed to her account was as yet untouched.

"He *is* good! he *is* kind and excellent!" she murmured to herself when, on his hurrying from the room after his usual fashion, to escape her thanks, she thought over his generosity— " and yet, how little have I deserved it !"

If this last reflection could but have been otherwise than transient—if the heart that his kindness had softened that hour, could but have retained its softness, Theresa might have been the best of wives, and made him the happiest of husbands; but it was not *in* her—it was not her character. Perhaps before the white cliffs of England had gladdened his sight, her heart had returned to its former state; and the goodness, kindness, and excellence of him who lay on the deck, prostrated by miserable suffering, and unable to entertain or attend to her, was effaced from it, and entirely forgotten—not perhaps for ever, but, (nearly as bad) for the time being.

CHAPTER VIII.

WHILST all these gay doings took place in Paris, preparations on the largest scale were going on in the quiet house in Hill Street, and almost from the hour that the wedding party had left its walls, that house might have been said to have been in a state of preparation.

Mrs. Chetwode never could be persuaded, even when she found that she was not to have her son and his wife with her at Christmas, that there would be time enough to get ready for them, so she had begun immediately after their departure.

New carpets in every room which Theresa was likely to enter were laid down;—new curtains were hung up in the drawing-room—between the windows mirrors were run up to enliven the whole, and every casual remark that Theresa had ever made had been carefully treasured up by Mrs. Chetwode, and brought into play now, as emblematical of her tastes, consequently to be acted on accordingly.

But the fever of these operations was nothing at all, compared to the state in which Mrs. Chetwode was thrown, when the letter arrived, announcing the actual day of their intended arrival.

She was in a tremble from morning till night, and tears rose to her eyes whenever Marian alluded to it, and to keep her thoughts and her body too, in constant movement, was the only cure which her daughter could think of for such unaccountable nervousness.

There was one part of Mark's latest letter to his mother which put the whole household very much out, and that was, his announcement that Victor being now his permanent servant, he trusted he might be accommodated in the house.

Every individual of that body of old and old-fashioned servants felt that the fine lady's maid of "young Mrs. Mark" was nothing at all to this!—Victor was disliked amongst them —there could be no doubt of that, for he had made them all feel small, as if they had been born in a world preceding this, and people do not like having their inferiority thrust before their eyes, after years and years of blissful ignorance.

However, there was no help for it; he was coming, and they must make room for him, so Mrs. Chetwode's own maid gave up her house-keeper's room down stairs, and with a very good grace saw it converted into a bed-room for Victor. In her heart she trembled at the introduction of a foreigner and a Papist, but the very air of that old house in Hill Street seemed to gift its inmates with charity, and they all complied to anything ordered by their mistress, in respectful silence.

" Marian," said Mrs. Chetwode, as, the day before the awful one, the mother and daughter sat and gazed at the new Aubusson carpet, the new furniture, and the new mirrors—" how very bright and strange everything looks !—I feel quite as if I were beginning a new life."

Marian smiled, for it would indeed be a new life to both of them, that steady house turned gay !

"And were it not for the Frenchman...it is very wrong of me to say so...I really think I might enjoy the idea of being what your Aunt Bellingham calls *stirred up !*"

And now the very evening itself arrived.

It rained, it poured, it snowed, it blew—in short the elements did everything they could do, and fires in all the rooms even, could hardly cheer up those who sat listening to the shaking of the windows, and the fitful howling of the wind.

It was no use listening to the carriage wheels, and expecting every set to stop at the door, for countless vehicles raced up and down the street incessantly, and on such a night it was not likely that any soul but some house-less beggar would be on foot.

And so Time wore on—who does not know all the sensations of such lingering moments? —who has not experienced the half faint, half chilly, half hungry, or rather, wretched, empty feelings with which the late dinner hour ap-proaches, arrives, and passes?

It was a known fact that whenever Mrs. and Miss Chetwode were suffering from any par-ticular emotion, all the domestics participated in it, to a certain degree. When Mark was going to be married, every servant was nervous beyond words;—there was not a steady hand in the house, the morning of the wedding, and

when they all assembled in the hall to bid him
goodbye, any one of them might have been
knocked down with less than a feather.

Consequently on this, the evening of his expected return, Mrs. Chetwode vacillated between Theresa's bedroom and the drawingroom,
so the butler and footman could not possibly
be expected to remain in the kitchen. The
former laid the table twenty times over to give
him an excuse for not leaving the diningroom,
and the latter was alternately concealed in the
hall, which was like an ice house, or located on
the first landing, drawing the lamp up and
down, pretending it did not burn weil. The
housemaid upset the coal scuttle twice on the
stairs, and Mrs. Chetwode's own maid was sta-
tioned in the dark at the turn of the banisters,
where she could have a good view.

How strange it is, that when an arrival of
great importance is to take place at a particular
house in a street, there are sure to be knocks
and stoppages at all the doors, right and left,

before the right knock comes at the right door.

But the time comes at last,—and at last the roll of one carriage, more rapid than the rest, and the shuffling of horse-hoofs, which never could have been caused by one quadruped, or even a pair, made Mrs. Chetwode hold her breath, and Marian run to the window.

The smoking horses hid the carriage, but it was stopping at the very door, and the lamps glared through the mist. Hastily up the stairs came a light and a heavy tread, and the next moment Mark and his wife were heartily welcomed by those who were so anxiously awaiting them.

People just off a journey are seldom attractive objects. Theresa, muffled up in furs, her cheeks pale with fatigue, and her long brown hair mingling with her sable tippet, dishevelled and out of curl, did not look like a brilliant bride, and Mark, hardly recovered from the effects of his voyage, was an object more of pity than admiration, so everyone went to their repose that night, disappointed.

There was but one who had not disappointed the high expections formed of him, and that was, Victor.

His figure was as fearfully tall—his cheeks were as strangely red, and his moustaches were as fiercely thick, as ever they were in days gone by; he was a hero still in fact, and too superior to the casualties of this life, to feel fatigue, or any other sort of 'ill that flesh is heir to,' as the antique saying goes.

He therefore waited at dinner that day, and had there been no other assistance, he could not have taken more upon himself.

Everywhere at once, yet noiseless, Mrs. Chetwode could only now and then catch sight of him, yet he waited upon all in turn, though he chiefly stood behind Theresa. Mrs. Chetwode's feeling of restraint in his presence was not unobserved by Mark, and he thought and hoped it would wear off when he had had an opportunity of detailing his many valuable qualities.

He determined in his own mind that unless Theresa particularly wished it, Victor should not wait at table another day, not at least until his mother had become accustomed to him, for his manners were so overpoweringly polite, in comparison with those who served with him, that Mark saw it was with the greatest difficulty the old lady could refrain from saying " Thank you" whenever he changed her plate, so completely did he clothe the action in the garb of the most courteous civility.

The first day after any great change, is always uncomfortable and unsettled ; we wake up with the question uppermost in our minds, " What has happened ?" but Theresa seemed just as much at home in the easy chair by the fire next day, as if she had occupied it as her place for months, instead of merely hours.

There was a pretty little third room off the drawing-rooms appropriated solely to her, so she was not obliged to "play company" all day, but this first day was cold, rainy, and dismal, and she therefore occupied the drawing-room, drew the largest chair she could find to the fire, and surrounding herself with books and magazines, read and slumbered, till luncheon.

Still the hours passed but slowly, and she found it fearfully dull after the constant gaiety and excitement of Paris; the day was too wet for Mrs. Chetwode to have her carriage out, and Theresa had as yet no horses, therefore she was tied to the house, and made no secret of the very great privation this was to her.

Mark had gone to his Temple chambers early, partly to see what had been going on in his absence, and partly to "look up" as he termed it, some of his great friends who were to be found in those regions.

He had but few to find, but those few were real friends, between whom and himself, subsisted the friendship of years, and he was welcomed with a sincere cordiality which quite warmed him up!

Before he had been ten minutes in the rooms of his particular ally, a Mr. Bathurst, the rest had gathered round him, and all expressed the strongest wish to become acquainted with Mrs. Mark.

Some were to call on the following Sunday, a grand visiting day for young barristers, and one or two were to dine in Hill Street at the end of the week, when the Chetwodes were a little more settled.

" In the mean time," said Bathurst, "come and dine with me the day after to-morrow—as many of you as can come, it shall be Chetwode's party, aud we will break up at ten precisely, in compliment to Benedict."

And the invitation was accepted as heartily as it was given.

As Chetwode walked home, the damp and the gloom around him could not chill the inward glow that good fellowship had filled him with, and he began thinking to himself how delightful it was to have such a prospect in store as an hour with Theresa before dinner, in which to tell her all his day's adventures;—so different to old times! his mother and sister knew all his friends so well, but to Theresa they would be new, and he should have to initiate her into the different character of each, and introduce her to them, a moment of pride to which he looked forward with impatient pleasure.

When he reached home, however, and hastily ascended to the drawing-room, no one was there but his mother and Marian, sitting over the fire in the dusk, hoping he would sit and chat with them for a few minutes, before Theresa came down—she had only gone to her room for some Eau de Cologne, as her head ached a little, and they expected her back every moment.

He sat down, half reluctantly, but he found he had very little to say—all the little chitchat that he had stored up for his wife, would be no news to his mother and sister, so he watched the minute hand of the clock as the fire in fitful flashes lighted it up, and counted ten, yet still Theresa was absent, and he rose, out of patience at last.

Just at that instant Victor entered.

" Madame would be very much obliged if Monsieur would join her in her own room."

And then Mark was provoked that he had not gone at first, without having delayed till he was sent for.

" Is that you?—*at last?*" enquired the languid voice as he entered in all haste.

" Yes, my dearest," and he hurried towards her as she lay on her sofa; " I thought you were coming down every moment, otherwise I should have come up directly."

" I never told any one I was coming down again—I had had quite enough of it! I assure you the dulness of that drawing-room, shut day, and no soul calling, not a knock or a ring even, was enough to give one the horrors!"

" To-morrow my dear Theresa, a pair of horses are to be sent for your approval—your time will not hang so heavily then."

" I hope not. Well? what have you been doing all day? are you to be absent every day in the week? I assure you I missed you, and shall hate those horrid chambers if you are to slave there from morning till night, like a law-yer's clerk—you might as well be a solicitor— I wonder you ever liked having a profession at all, when there is no necessity for it."

" My dearest, I should be lost without my profession; remember it was my sole variety...' began Chetwode.

" Yes, *it was*," interrupted Theresa; " but you have a wife to attend to now; well, but you have not told me what you have been doing? tell me how every moment has been spent since we parted, a hundred years ago, *at least!*"

More flattered than vexed by these petulant little speeches, Mark began relating all that had befallen him amongst his friends: he expatiated on their good qualities, spoke of the pride and pleasure it would be to him to introduce them to Theresa—dwelt with delight on the agreeable house he could now ask them to, and particularly engaged Theresa's good graces beforehand for his friend Bathurst.

Theresa owned that her taste was very fastidious, so she could not promise, but what was he like? was he young or old?

" Older than I am, and good-looking, but when you know him you will be sure to like him for himself; he is a rising man, and has slaved all his life, as you just remarked, more than any lawyer's clerk!"

" Then I shall not like him—I hate drones."

"But Bathurst is anything but a drone; he is full of life and spirits, and enjoys himself out of school like any boy: he has asked me to dine with him the day after to-morrow, to meet two more of my old friends."

Chetwode paused as if for Theresa's answer, but she made none; he looked at her, and there was a cloud on her brow.

"You will spare me, Theresa?" asked he, doubtfully, yet hardly believing that the cloud could have been caused by anything he had said. On this point, however, he was speedily undeceived.

"It is a very good joke," began his wife, in her coldest and most sarcastic voice, "to ask me that, after you have actually accepted the invitation!"

"I did not say that I had accepted it," returned Mark, mildly, "I said that he had asked me, but if you can show any just cause or impediment, Theresa, why—"

"Oh, dear no!" interrupted Theresa, rising; "pray let us have no jokes on the subject; I am the worst person in the world for a joke on subjects which I consider serious, therefore if, according to your notions of propriety, a newly married man may leave his wife in the strange home that he has brought her to, within the first week of her arrival, and join a merry-making of bachelor friends—*pray go!*"

" But, my dearest, these friends of mine are not a merry-making set."

" Well—they *may* be, and they may *not* be."

" But I give you my word they are *not*, Theresa !"

" Then I suppose I must believe you; but that does not alter the case; go, by all means, and show them that they have not lost one of their convivial band, although in *outward* profession, he has left them !"

" This is hardly fair," said Mark, after a silence of a few moments; " I cannot see how so trifling a sacrifice to my pleasure can so displease you—but if indeed you are displeased, Theresa, nothing shall induce me to go to Bathurst's on Thursday. I will write an apology this very evening;" and he advanced towards her writing-table.

"You may do as you like, of course," said Theresa; "but do not give out to your friends that *I* prevented you!—do not stay at home on my account, I beg."

"My Theresa, this is not amiable," were the low-toned words breathed by Mark, as his pen passed rapidly over the paper; "yet I cannot bring myself to believe you mean to act unkindly; there, there is my note—read what I have said."

And she read—

"Dear Bathurst,

"I am afraid you must excuse my dining with you on Thursday, for on my return home I found an engagement, which I cannot put off. Do not, however, forget yours to us on Friday.

Sincerely yours,

Mark Chetwode.

"He will see through that," exclaimed

Theresa; " he will say in a moment that I did not like your dining out with these gay bachelors."

" Would he be wrong?" asked Mark, with a half smile.

" It is no business of his," she began.

Mark took the note quietly out of her hands and threw it into the fire.

" Dictate, my dear Theresa," said he.

" Not I," she returned; " but why do you not just say, that since you parted you are quite sorry to find you are prevented keeping your engagement with him?'

Nearly verbatim the words were written, the note was sent to the post, and Chetwode rose with a sigh.

" You are a good boy," said his wife, taking his hand, and carrying it to her lips as he passed her, " but I am sorry a little sacrifice to oblige me, cost you such a sigh."

" Dear Theresa," was his answer as he left he room, " *it was not the sacrifice.*"

When that note reached Mr. Bathurst he immediately postponed his party; they had only been invited to meet Chetwode, so they easil consented to hold themselves engaged for som future day, when he would be able to make one of their number.

All that evening Theresa was in the highes spirits, and the greatest good humour. Mrs. Chetwode was quite pleased, for she had fancied, somehow, from her manner in the morning, that the dulness of the day had depressed her.

" How beautiful she is !" said she to her son, when Theresa was out of hearing—" how beautiful and how improved !—what a prize you have won !"

And Mark's placid smile was the only reply he made.

The next day, according to the orders he had given, a pair of young greys were brought up to the stables, and being put to Theresa's carriage, were driven up and down opposite the windows, for her verdict.

They were fine showy horses, with the high action so apt to captivate a lady's taste, and she was charmed, but Mark thought they did not look very steady ;—one of them showed a decided disinclination to pass anything, and stood in a fidgetty, restless way, when drawn up before the door.

" All spirits sir—no vice," said the horse-dealer who sat by Mrs. Chetwode's old coachman on the box—" just up from grass, sir—only want a few hours' work."

" What is *your* opinion Roberts ?" asked Chetwode of the old coachman ; " they are for Mrs. Mark, and I am particularly anxious she should have a very steady pair."

" Too young to be over steady, sir," was the old man's answer; " but they seem safe enough —pretty action that young one, sir."

Yes—there could not be a doubt about the beauty of their paces, and after much persuasion Mark was tempted to believe that all the restlessness of action and eye which alarmed him, was only from their being very fresh.

The dealer asked for one day, and promised to turn them out the next, on trial, as quiet as lambs, for he declared that a lady could drive them when they were on regular work, so it was thus arranged, and Theresa was overjoyed and enraptured.

Her own horses!—what happiness! and the very pair in all the world that she should have chosen; how she should ever have patience to wait until the next day, was a mystery to her, and her delight was as exuberant as that of a child.

" How natural she is!" exclaimed her mother-in-law, rejoicing to see her so thoroughly and unaffectedly happy; " how few, Mark, would show their pleasure in that joyous, sparkling manner! it does one good to hear her laugh, and in these days of self-control, one seldom hears that ringing sound, except in a child."

And Mark, at the bottom of his heart, fervently wished that that buoyancy were not so evanescent!

The next day accordingly, at the appointed hour, the carriage, driven, for that occasion, by Mrs. Chetwode's coachman, came to the door, and then took one turn, the greys pacing proudly along, and champing their bits impatiently.

The old coachman watched them with a keen eye, though he held them with a light hand, and certainly when they returned to the door they stood quiet enough, so Theresa got in, followed by her husband, a measure she did not approve, because she thought men were so out of place in carriages, though she had not offered any violent opposition.

First they drove round Hyde Park, and all went well; then they entered the Regent's Park, and still for speed and *showyness*, no horses could have better pleased their delighted mistress.

" You see!" she exclaimed, " you see how

quietly they go! now do let us vary the scene a little, and go into the streets."

" Where would you go?" asked Mark.

" Down Regent-street, and round, and home that way."

And the order was given. They therefore turned into Park-crescent, and entered Portland-place. As they approached Regent-street, a huge cart, covered with enormous red placards came in sight, and slowly advancing, filled the minds of the young greys with frightful visions.

First they shyed—then plunged, and finally, feeling that the master-hand compelled them to pass, they gave one bolt in unison, and starting off, dashed across Oxford-street, and down the busy thoroughfare at an ungovernable pace.

On they went—every one stopping, and looking after them, as if awaiting the catastrophe, and it was very soon evident that all control over them was gone;—the coachman could do nothing but endeavour to guide their almost flying course, and trust that chance might interpose some barrier to check them before any collision occurred. At the corner of Piccadilly, however, the intemperate career closed, for the off-horse made an abrupt attempt to turn, and losing his footing, owing to the slippery state of the streets, fell to the ground, dragging his companion over him.

All this time Theresa and her husband had sat speechless; her teeth were closely set together, and her hands clenched in the holders of the carriage, whilst he awaited, with a sort of desperate calmness, the crisis.

When this arrived, he sprang out without an instant's delay, and Theresa, trembling in every limb, yet declaring that she was not the least frightened, half walked and was half carried into Swan and Edgar's shop.

So ended the adventure of that day, and all the rest of it Mark had to listen to asseverations on the part of his wife, which he knew were very far from the truth, namely, that no blame could be attached to the horses, but that the old coachman alone was in fault, he not having had strength to hold them in.

" I don't mean to say, dear Mrs. Chetwode," she began at dinner, " that he is not a good coachman, but I mean that he is very old, you know ; he may do perfectly for your nice, fat, steady horses, but here are a pair of high-bred, high-spirited creatures, that must require a firmer hand."

" The horses are imperfectly broken," said Mark, " I saw it the moment they moved."

" But can they not be broken in again ?" persisted Theresa, " anything in the world but change them !—I have fixed my heart on those horses, Mark, and shall be miserable if you deny them to me !"

" I would deny you nothing as you well know," was her husband's answer, " were it not that I consider them positively dangerous ; my dearest Theresa, I should never have a happy moment were I away from you, and knew that you were out with these unlucky greys."

" Ah, you will get over that! will he not, Mrs. Chetwode? After I have come home alive five or six times, you will forget your idea, that I shall be brought home dead!"

Chetwode almost shuddered at her words; so dreadful an idea had never occurred to him, it was too painful to realize or even image, but his opinion was unshaken, and he earnestly wished the horses to be returned.

Theresa's cry however was still, No, no, no! and at last she gained the day, more by chance than importunity, for the fact was, fond and fervent hopes for a future heir to the house of Chetwode were dawning, and Mrs. Chetwode implored her son, by looks, and hints, and shakes of the head, not to thwart or *contrarier* the precious being, whose will and pleasure was sure to be always in opposition to whatever was right and prudent.

Mark therefore submitted, but with an ill grace, and as the horses were uninj red, they were returned to be better broken, an indefinite answer only, being given with them, so that they were not actually purchased.

On the Friday, Theresa, being still in high good humour, was rather in a state of excitement to see Mr. Bathurst, and begged her sister-in-law to tell her exactly, what he was like.

" Mark says he is good looking; you know my horror of ugly people!—it was born with me, and no fault of mine, so tell me, is he so?"

" More pleasing than handsome," said Marian, " but there is something very agreeable about him: I believe he is likely to be a distinguished man, for he is exceedingly clever."

" I am not sure that I like clever people— but Mark has a very high opinion of him, has he not?"

" Yes, of his judgment as well as his talents; he has always been his greatest friend, and I do not know any one who has so much influence over him, for he used to consult him, on all occasions."

This was not a fortunate speech. Marian should have put the influence into the past tense, for what wife likes to hear, that there is any one, except herself, who possesses " much influence" over her husband? To Theresa the remark was extremely disagreeable, and she immediately suspected Marian of *malice prepense*, and made a memorandum in her own mind, that the influence should now cease.

She wondered whether Mark had consulted him on the occasion of his marriage, but she did not like to ask—she was too proud—however the impressions regarding Mr. Bathurst, which had till then been very favorable, now received a considerable check, and Theresa was much more inclined to dislike him, than to admire and approve.

That afternoon Theresa went out driving with Mrs. Chetwode, not calling on any of her friends, because the cream-coloured chariot was too odious for that, but taking a drive, synonymous with " doing penance," and on their return, a circumstance had occurred, which discomposed the whole party.

Victor and the ancient butler had "had words," as servants say, and Mrs. Chetwode found both in such an irate and indignant temper when, she was called upon to interpose her authority, that she in her turn, requested Theresa to be the mediator, and whatever Theresa wished should be done, for Mark was not at home to be consulted.

The cause of the dispute arose when Victor, with his imperfect knowledge of English, volunteered to assist in laying the dinner-table, and commenced a long harangue, in the most incomprehensible mixture of languages, to explain to his superior, the foreign and last-introduced mode of so doing.

At this period, the now prevalent custom of not removing the table-cloth at dessert, had not been generally adopted by the middling classes of society, but was chiefly confined to those lordly halls, where every dish was handed, and none helped, and damask of rare beauty kept its place till the guests themselves had departed.

But in France, the fashion was universal, and at a certain stage of the ceremony when the table was about to be decorated, Victor after looking round him for several minutes suddenly ejaculated—

" Where your *sleeps* ?"

When, after much time lost in vain conjecture, the butler comprehended that the question referred to " slips " to lay down each side of the table, he explained that there were no such things in the house ; that his mistress's mahogany tables were far too beautiful to be hidden, and then Victor threw out contemptuous observations on the old-fashioned system, which roused the ancient man to retort with some asperity.

Victor hinted, in better English than usual, that perhaps the table linen in Hill-street would not bear the examination, which was rather courted than otherwise, by the custom of

France, and he received for answer that "*foreigneers*" had not a table in all their country fit to be shown, so the cuts were equally severe on both sides, and when the two mistresses returned home, the process of laying the dinner table was in *statu quo*, and the belligerents awaiting an umpire.

Theresa then, being appointed that umpire, unhesitatingly decided on Victor's side, and a second table-cloth was converted into "*sleeps*," to the triumph of one man, and the ill-concealed anger of the other.

"If this is to be the order of the day, and *foreigneers* to take the lead, I'm of no use," was the observation with which the latter descended to the spheres below, and Mrs. Chetwode trembled upstairs, full of fears lest she should have to receive his resignation, before the day had closed.

Mark, when the dispute was reported to him, was exceedingly annoyed, and vexed at the part Theresa had taken.

" Manners is so valuable to my mother," said he, "that were he to give warning, I really do not know what she would do!—I am sincerely sorry, Theresa, that you decided on Victor's side, particularly as we had no slips belonging to us, for it was only setting Manners against us!"

" Better than affronting Victor," replied Theresa.

" Why not change even now?" asked her husband, " anything better than hurting the feelings of the poor old man."

" What, *now?* give them all the trouble over again?—my dear Mark, how absurd!— no, leave it as it is for to-day, and next time let Manners have it his fashion; tell him so, and the wounded feelings will soon heal," so Mark summoned the crestfallen functionary and kindly assured him it was only a trial, and that next time it should all be as it had ever been.

CHAPTER IX.

" Master's the same as ever!" said the worthy
butler to the housekeeper, as they stood and
l ooked at the novel appearance of the double
table-cloth together, "just the same at heart,
but it's a pity he gives way to Mrs. Mark; he
ain't half firm enough!—why should I mind
the trouble of laying the cloth over again?—
wouldn't I have laid it a hundred times in an
hour, to see the table look as well as it used?—
but it's done now, and never in this world will
it go back again to the old way!—master says,

'next time!' bless his heart, just to comfort me, but I know better; it never will!"

And the old butler was right.—Once adopt a new system, patronised by one powerful voice, and you will never return into the old path again.

Mark Chetwode need not have been so anxious that evening, that Theresa should look her best in the eyes of his friends, for she had enough vanity in her composition to be determined that they should approve his choice, and besides being more particular than usual about her appearance, she was also in the humour to make herself as agreeable as she could.

When Mr. Bathurst was announced, the dim light of the room allowed of her giving him more than a cursory glance, and she was disappointed, as we always are when we have heard much of a person. He was "nothing to look at," as the saying is; merely gentlemanly, with manners as perfectly at ease, and as lively, as her husband's were quiet and shy.

What on earth was there about this man, thought she to herself, that he should have gained "much influence" over one who seemed so very much older in mind, in habits, and in everything, than himself, for Mark looked ten years more than his actual age.

But before Theresa had been an hour in his company, the spell began to operate, and the reason of his influence became evident. He did not utter a word that was not worth listening to; he did not detail the most simple anecdote, but what it was worth remembering, and the man of talent shone out, in spite of the most light-hearted and careless exterior.

Still Theresa *would* not like him! Mark listened to him too reverently—submitted to him too deferentially, and asked his opinion on too many points, for her to like him, and her whole study, all dinner time, was, to show that her husband required no superior power except herself—that he spoke her sentiments, judged with her judgment, and saw with her eyes.

Bathurst suspected something of this before he had conversed many moments, and his quick, shrewd eye glanced from one to the other with a rapid yet scrutinizing movement, but on his friend's mild face there was an expression of such perfect happiness, and contentment, that he fancied he must be mistaken in the idea that had first arisen in his mind, and that what he had not at first particularly liked, was merely a little assumption of authority, which rather became, than otherwise, so beautiful a creature.

He narrowly watched the elder Mrs. Chetwode too, and he remarked that at every word that fell from those attractive lips, a proud and a delighted smile, played on the old lady's face, so he determined to like Mrs. Mark, as well as to admire her, for as to her claims to admiration there could not be two opinions.

In the course of the evening, as the party found themselves seated in sociable groups about various parts of the room, Mr. Bathurst, as Mark's most intimate, friend, tried to improve his acquaintance with the young wife, and drew his chair to her side with the easy, unceremonious air of *l'ami de la maison.*

Theresa did not much approve this; she was reclining in a *chaise longue,* and considering that she had sufficiently exerted herself during dinner, she was not much disposed to talk conversation any more; a large fan was in her hand, and she preferred looking at the fire to looking at Mr. Bathurst's face.

Mark saw the state of affairs and, came to the rescue, taking up that place on the hearth-rug so exclusively monopolised by Englishmen —that place in the centre which so effectually screens the fire from the rest of the company, and only leaves to the freezing, the alternative of the hob.

Mr. Bathurst happened to be speaking at the time.

" I am not fond of Dorsetshire as a county,"

he was saying—"but feeling like a bird out of its cage, I enjoyed the little I saw of it."

"I was there some months in the summer," said Theresa in an indolent voice, "and never thought the world held such a lovely spot as where *I* was staying!—where were you?"

"I was at your cousins'—the Rydals'," and Mr. Bathurst turned towards Mark—"I went down for a few days shooting, and stayed three weeks!—the nicest people on the face of the earth!—by the bye, I met Rydal in town just after you accepted my invitation to dinner, and if you had not played me false, he would have been one of our party. Mrs Chetwod,eyou have no idea what a shabby fellow your husband is; he promised to dine with me, made me ask a jovial few to meet him, and then, sent me an excuse!"

Theresa glanced up at her husband, and her lip curled, but she said nothing. Mark felt that look, and wished his friend had left out the expression, "jovial few," for unfortunately, though it was used in jest, he knew that she would take it in earnest.

By way of apology, he mentioned the fright his wife had had with her new horses, and said that even had he not previously sent an excuse, he should not have been able to join the party after such an adventure.

"You never told me you wanted carriage horses," said Bathurst, after listening attentively to the story, "why did you not let me know?"

Theresa could have replied "because we did not see the necessity;" but she satisfied herself with merely sneering, and in her heart, disliking the officious friend more than ever.

"I did not think you could help me," answered Mark, "so I went at once to * * *" naming the dealer who had served him—"I do not say that the man is in fault," he added, "but the horses are too young, and too skittish."

"For skittish, read spirited," said Theresa, rising with some vehemence from her recumbent position; "my husband, Mr. Bathurst, is dreadfully timid—" and she sank back again with a gesture of contempt and petulance, the vehemence subsiding instantly, as though it were too much trouble to retain anything but the outward expression of it, in her sparkling eyes.

" At all events, I wish I had known," repeated Bathurst, "for there were a pair in the market the other day, worth their weight in gold— Cornwall's greys," said he, again appealing to his friend.

" Cornwall selling his horses ? I never heard of Cornwall selling a horse in my life. Where is he now ? for I have lost sight of him, and he was one of the best fellows that ever lived."

" Ah; we shall not have him amongst us again. He has lost a great deal of money, and gone abroad to economise ; you must remember those fine animals he used to drive in his curricle? Mrs. Cornwall might have driven them herself.

But he means to part with his whole stud, from sheer inability to keep even the favourites."

Mark was attracted by this information, and made many minute inquiries, as to where he could see them—what was asked for them, and if they were available immediately?

His questions were all satisfactorily answered, and he turned towards Theresa full of anxiety to go the very next day, and secure the prizes.

But on her countenance of immoveable gravity, sat a look of such firm determination. that no sooner had his eyes rested on it than he saw a storm was brewing. There was a lowering look on those features, when anything displeasing had occurred, which reminded one of the appearance of the atmosphere, when there is thunder in the air.

To his animated address, she paused before she vouchsafed any answer, and then, raising her large white eyelids, slowly and scornfully, she said,

" You have given Mr. Bathurst the trouble of descanting on the merits of these faultless horses, and forgotten in return, to give him an important piece of information, which is—that we are suited."

"But—" persisted Chetwode, too anxious to be easily daunted; " I gave a very indefinite answer to * * *; there would be no difficulty in resigning this uncomfortable pair, in favour of those belonging to Cornwall—independently of the satisfaction it would be to me, to add my mite towards extricating so old a friend from his difficulties; I should be very glad of so fair an opportunity for relieving my mind of a constant source of terror and anxiety."

Theresa smiled.

" As I told you before," said she, with cool indifference, " you are dreadfully timid—quite absurd. Of course, if you wish to purchase these horses out of charity, it is no affair of mine :. we shall only have a pair a-piece, in that case. They will take you to the Temple and back—and perhaps Mr. Bathurst is also authorized to put the curricle up for sale; we should then never interfere with each other. But as far as *I* am concerned, I have no wish for any horses but those we have selected."

Mark's colour had risen to crimson during this speech; he tried to laugh, but it was so forced a sound, that it was painful to hear it. He tried to carry off the sarcasms as though they were playful jokes; but he was a bad actor, and the assumed gaiety with which he said,

"You see, Bathurst, I am under orders," was a mockery of mirth, and impressed his friend most disagreeably. Chetwode saw that it did, and his evening was spoilt. The happiness of the early part of it was damped, and though he was not yet alive to all the humiliation of being "snubbed before company," as children call it, still, he was mortified at the tone Theresa had adopted, and would have given anything rather than that Bathurst should be witness to one cloud on that brow, or hear one word from those lips (which he himself still tried to believe spoke nothing but pearls) which might not impress him in her favour.

And certainly, when Bathurst took his leave that evening, he was not pre-possessed; the two friends who had accompanied him were in raptures; they thought Chetwode the luckiest fellow in the world, but he who had looked beyond the external loveliness, who did not care for luxuriance of ringlets and witchery of eyes, felt saddened, without being quite able to answer to himself why he was so.

To the raillery of his companions, as to whether the bright lot of their quondam ally had made him look in, repining, upon the darkness and loneliness of his own heart, he tried to give back an answer in the same spirit—for even to them he did not like to say, that he doubted whether Chetwode might not some day prove more an object of pity, than envy.

He had searched beyond that fair outside, and though he did not deny the perfection of the features, the first thing that had struck him was the exceedingly unpleasing expression they bore.

Her voice too was not of that tone which has been pronounced " a very excellent thing in woman," and, unfortunately, in the discussion about the horses, a display so very nearly approaching to temper had been exhibited, that on the whole, his high expectations were considerably lessened, and he feared that his friend's judgment had certainly been slightly influenced, by his admiration.

Perhaps, in Hill-street, the impression he had himself made, might not have been called any more favourable, for Theresa preserved the most obstinate silence, until called upon by her husband to speak, and then the "faint praise," which has been pronounced as more condemnatory than even censure, chilled Chetwode more, than if she had openly said, she disliked him.

The next morning, however, when as usual, Mark had forgotten that the rose-leaves had been a little ruffled the evening before, he unfortunately began again at breakfast, on the subject of his friend, Colonel Cornwall's, greys, and asked Theresa if she would like them sent up in the course of the day, for inspection.

Her veto was given, without an instant's hesitation. She had no wish to inspect them; it was only giving unnecessary trouble, and perhaps raising hopes that could not fail to be disappointed, seeing that her own mind was made up to have none but those she had already tried and approved.

It was almost a pity, now that the system of yielding had continued in force so long, that Chetwode, on this occasion, was importunate, for it only convinced his wife still more of the necessity of checking Mr. Bathurst's influence, and made her more resolved not to give way;

but Mark felt so deep an interest in the misfortunes of those whom he esteemed, that he actually did not see how rapidly Theresa's temper was rising, and how very soon, if he were not warned, it would come to a downright dispute.

A scene like that impending, it must be remembered, was perfectly new to Mrs. Chetwode, *mère*; she had not the remotest idea but that her son's wishes were her daughter-in-law's guides, and that Theresa's will, was, by the same reasoning, Mark's law, for she thought one never wished, what the other did not feel was an answering sentiment to some hidden feeling of their own.

Consequently, the motherly fears that had prompted her on another occasion to entreat Mark not to thwart his young wife, now impelled her to caution him not to allow any little discussion to agitate or excite her; so one by one the whole four were soon engaged in an animated conversation, rather too warm to be called amicable, for the few words which Marian occasionally added, were more calculated to defend her brother, than her sister-in-law.

Of Marian's interference, Theresa took not the slightest notice; she looked upon her as a sort of nonentity, whose remarks had some-what of the same weight as "the idle wind," but at the same time she did not intend Mark's yielding to be owing to his mother's interecs-sion; he must bow to her, and her alone, and after words had risen as high as it was possible, the husband gave up the struggle.

"Then, my dear Theresa, it shall be as you wish—the pair on which you have set your heart shall be yours, and now it only remains for me to let Bathurst know."

Mark spoke in the depressed voice which he now so often accidentally assumed, and though his wife took no notice of it, it touched his mother's heart, and she could not resist saying —"Perhaps if you and dear Theresa were to talk it over a little more."

But to this Theresa instantly exclaimed—
"Oh, dear no—why should we talk on a subject on which my mind is made up?—I assure
you, Mrs. Chetwode, I am not a vacillating
disposition;—what I say I mean,—so Mark
must do as he likes, now that he knows my
resolution."

"Then now I shall go to Bathurst," said
he.

"And why?" asked Theresa, whose irritability seized every possible pretext for explosion.

"To let him know our determination."

"Why must he know?—what has he to do
with it?"

"My dearest!—when he it was that told me
of these horses?"

"I know—but what does it signify to him?
—why need Mr. Bathurst have anything to do
with our domestic arrangements?—I consider
it very impertinent of *any one* to interfere in
them in *any way!*"

At these words, Mrs Chetwode, who was

standing by the fire, quietly left the room, and
it was not long before Marian followed her, and
then Mark spoke rather hastily.

"Pray, Theresa, did you mean that at my
mother and sister?"

" If they ever interfere, of which you are
the best judge, they may apply it to themselves
if they like; but as to Mr. Bathurst, what possible right has he to interfere between you
and me?"

" My dearest!" exclaimed Chetwode, exceedingly provoked, " you really are enough to put
one out of temper!—what is it you wish?
what is it you mean?—how on earth has Bathurst interfered between you and me?"

" In wishing you to buy horses recommended
by himself, when he knew that I had fixed my
heart on others; I call that interfering! then
again, before we had been three days in town,
did he not try to draw you into a bachelor

party to dine with him, and a set, whom he pleased to term 'a jovial few?'"

"He was joking," said Mark.

"At all events the invitation was in earnest," retorted Theresa.

Chetwode said no more; he took off his gloves and the warm muffler which he had tied round his throat in preparation of a cold walk, and ringing the bell, he ordered a cab to be sent for to take him to the Temple; thus tacitly informing Theresa that he had given up the idea of going to Bathurst's.

But though he submitted almost without resistance, many disagreeable feelings were revived by the scene just enacted; the hopes that he had nourished of a new leaf turned over, were drooping; the happy anticipations he had formed during the first day or two of their arrival in town, were dashed to the ground; he now saw the disposition he had to deal with, and though he loved her too devotedly to regret the step he had taken in joining his life with hers, still rebellious thoughts would sometimes arise in moments of great annoyance, and he would try, strenuously, *not* to embody those thoughts in the bitter words—

" I should have been happier—*unmarried!*"

Sometimes he tried to think it was his own fault; that he did not know how to manage her, for certainly there were none of these scenes (as far as he knew) between her, and her mother; sometimes he fancied it might be a peculiar and temporary irritability, but her sweetness at other times, when no rose-leaves were ruffled, contradicted this; then it would occur to him—an idea wretched enough to embitter his whole existence, present and future—that he had not made himself sufficiently sure of her affections before they married; that that fatal worldly prosperity which one, more fitted to win her heart, did *not* possess, might have been used by her worldly mother as an incentive to the sacrifice, and might have even blinded her own young judgment, to the danger of the step she was taking.

Yet to whom could Chetwode impart these harrowing fears?—who was there who could relieve this torturing dread of years to come? To his mother he would not speak—for *now*, the days recurred to his memory when the hesitation with which she had given her consent, had failed to show him that she had her fears for his happiness, though now, alas! his eyes were opened, and he construed her reluctant manner, aright.

To Marian, how could he venture to speak on the subject?—had he not often tried in vain to forget the firm yet gentle manner in which she had opposed his predilection, even in its earliest stage? Did he not well remember, after that *tête-á-tête* dinner at Mrs. Bellingham's, his memorable conversation with his sister, in which she confessed, that she also, had heard all that had been told him, against the Derings and Theresa, *and did not disbe-lieve it.*

How then could he speak to her?—Lastly, there was his friend Bathurst; he who had till now been his guide, his counsellor, and his refuge in all dilemmas;—to him he *dared* not speak!—Against that once unlimited confidence an interdict had been placed—Bathurst was restricted from any share in anything "*do-mestic!*"—Even though Theresa might never know it, still her words had sunk deeply into her husband's heart, and he recollected too well that the slightest communication within the limits of the word "domestic," would come under the denomination of "imper-tinent!" so from this communion of friendship, once so unreserved, he was now restricted, by a law to which he had consented by silence!

It may be said, or inferred, from these many proofs, that the disposition of Mark Chetwode was devoid of all that firmness of mind and purpose, which invests a husband with power to assert at least his own dignity, but this was not actually the case; the great misfortune of his character was unconquerable love of ease—unconquerable love of peace and quiet, and to attain these, he thought no sacrifice too great.

He never, till now, looked forward to the incalculable mischief which this principle might produce, were he associated with one who would take advantage of the weakness; but now that the poison was beginning to work—that he had once given the reins into hands able and determined to hold them—that he had once, in short, given way, rather than offer opposition,—he felt that the 'vantage ground had slid from beneath him,—that he could never more regain the mastery,—but that henceforth the system must go on, day by day, and year by year, growing in strength, and increasing in misery, until he himself should have no more mental strength, than present power, to withstand it !—

A few days after this, Bathurst overtook Mark on his way to the Temple, and seemed

so glad to have secured his arm, that instead
of proceeding, each to his own chambers, they
turned in a contrary direction, and wandered
on, looking into the shop windows and enjoying themselves like boys out of school, till
suddenly, the former recollected his friend's
broken engagement, and asked him to fix some
day, were it even in a month's time, when he
would promise to dine with him.

No question could have been much more unlucky!—During the whole of that walk, Chetwode's manner had been abstracted at intervals,
and thoughts of Theresa were constantly presenting themselves in every possible form, and
not agreeably.

In the first place, he thought to himself how
he had once looked forward with all joyousness, to saying to his friend, " How do you like
my wife ?" and now that the time had arrived,
he had not been able to put the question!—he
longed to do it, yet something held him back
—he could not frame the words !—he dreaded

some reply which would fall short of his own exaggerated wishes, and he felt by force of long habit, that if Bathurst disapproved his choice, the disapproval would have some weight; Bathurst's words were oracles—his influence was, as yet, undiminished—so he had talked on all sorts of indifferent subjects, till he had led the conversation into quite a different direction.

Then again, another uncomfortable idea possessed him, and that was, that he should not like to meet Theresa whilst he was taking this *tête-à-tète* walk with his friend, because he had told her that he was going to his chambers—he felt certain it would be made the ground of some unpleasant recrimination, so no sooner had they gained one of the entrances to Hyde Park, than, without giving any reason, he insisted on turning short off, and retracing their steps into Piccadilly.

From all these conflicting thoughts, the question and invitation of Bathurst recalled him to himself, and he evaded it by every means in his power; he knew it was no use accepting! he should only have to go home and write a note of apology—just act the scene over again—so he gave the answer which comes in so aptly when one does not exactly know what to say, and told his friend that he " would let him know!"

" By the bye, how do your horses answer?" was the next query; " have you bought them?"

" Yes—I have; my wife had set her heart on them, so I gave way; but my new coachman, though he has as strong a hand as any I ever saw, tells me it is as much as he can do sometimes, to hold them in; the fact is, they were not properly broke, in the first instance and they do not forget it; however, Theresa is pleased, and that is everything."

" True; poor Cornwall's are not sold yet, I am sorry to say—I think he asked too much."

Mark thought to himself how gladly he would have given to the " uttermost farthing " but he said nothing.

By this time they had reached that part of Piccadilly where vehicles most congregate, and where the ground ascends gradually towards Hatchett's. As they advanced, they saw a crowd in the distance, and on approaching, their progress was completely stopped, by a mass of people crushing and crowding round one spot, over which policemen were flinging saw-dust.

" Some accident !" exclaimed Bathurst with all the excitement, (looking very much like delight,) which invariably animates an Englishman on these occasions, " what has happened ?"

Each individual composing that crowd, had of course his own peculiar version of the accident, but the story in its simplest form appeared to be, that a pair of horses had taken fright ; they were attached to a barouche, in which was one lady only ; they had started at the corner of the Regent Circus, and had pursued their reckless course until opposite Hatchett's, where one of them had come in furious contact with a gig, one of the shafts of which pierced the chest of the horse, and injured it so severely, that it had been destroyed on the spot.

Thus the saw-dust, and the crowd, and the policemen, were all accounted for, and the two friends pursued their way to their club.

Strange to say, the accident, beyond eliciting some expressions of pity and regret from Chetwode, excited no other feelings; but on his friend, it made an impression which he could not shake off—it filled him with a sort of vague fear that they should hear of it again, and he suddenly exclaimed in surprise—

" Only think of our never inquiring to whom the carriage belonged!"

" I asked if anyone was hurt," said Chetwode, turning into the club, " and they said no; —any letters for me?"

There were no letters, but the porter asked if Mr. Chetwode had met his servant?

" Servant?—no—what servant?"

" Your valet, sir—he has not been gone a

minute—a foreigner, sir—and as far as I could
make out, you were wanted directly."

" Now what on earth," began Mark deliberately, as he quietly took off his hat, and
threw down his gloves, " what on earth could
Victor want with me ?"

How strange it is, that sometimes no fore-
shadow of evil, prepares those whom it most
concerns, to meet it, whilst others, far less
interested, take alarm instantly.

So it was with Chetwode and his friend.
The prompt and active nature of Bathurst,
was all on the alert, before Mark's second glove
was off, and he had actually called a cab,
dragged him downstairs, and hurried him into
it, before the latter could ask the faintest explanation.

" Ask nothing," cried Bathurst, " only go
home—you hear that your man has gone on to
the Temple to find you, and you hear that he
was in a cab; these desperate measures are not
taken for nothing, and I would not seek to

alarm you, did I not see how very slow you are to take fire; if I have hurried you needlessly, laugh at me by-and bye, but if *pour cause,* you will only thank me."

And telling the driver to make the best of his way to Hill Street, Bathurst watched the cab out of sight, and re-entered the club, satisfied that it was going at its utmost speed.

But by this time Mark *had* begun to feel anxious; though he endeavoured to shut out from his view, the vision of the remains of the accident in Piccadilly, yet still it would rise, mixing itself up in his mind, and making him painfully restless and uneasy;—he tried to reason with himself, and ask why that scene should haunt him so, but he only grew more and more nervous, till, sick with apprehension as he reached Hill Street, he sprang from the cab, and darted into his house.

That the door was already open, did not attract his attention; all he saw, on hastening through the hall, was Marian, waiting for him on the stairs, and rushing down as he advanced, she chilled his very blood, and almost nailed him to the spot by the words—

" Thank God! dearest Mark, she is not hurt!—it was only the horse—Theresa was brought home in a private carriage, and she is only frightened, not the least hurt!"

CHAPTER X.

IT was true that by the fearful accident—that very accident of which Chetwode had so narrowly escaped being a witness—his late and valuable purchase of the " skittish " horse only, had fallen a victim; but Theresa had received at the same time a shock which was productive of the most serious consequences and the hopes of the Chetwodes were dashed to the ground.

Stretched on a bed of sickness, the tenderness of those around her was called into active

play, and yet it was many weeks before she
recovered either health or spirits, for the memory of the fright she had sustained preyed on
her mind, and in describing the accident she said
that from the moment the horses first broke
into their ungovernable pace she recollected
nothing, until the last crash came; " but," she
always added in conclusion, " it was not the
fault of the horses; something startled them;
they were going beautifully at the time, and I
only hope, dear Mark, if you have any love for
me, you will try and match the one that is
left !"

Long before Mark Chetwode had recovered
his serenity, the more elastic spirits of his
young wife regained their force, and she was
fluttering about again as wild, as wilful, and as
brilliant as ever.

He found it impossible to forget the narrow
escape he had had of losing her, neither could
he get over the disappointment of hopes that
had often buoyed him up in the midst of cir-

cumstances depressing to a degree; neither
could he look now at those beautiful features
without many an inward prayer of gratitude
for her deliverance.

Considering all things, and considering also
the great influence she already possessed over
him, it was almost a pity that an escape so narrow as to endear her to him tenfold, should
just then have occurred!

He never for an instant thought of her wilfulness, her perversity and her temper altogether—that was all forgotten in that boundless
sentiment of gratitude to Heaven for having
spared her to him, so when she again shone
upon his existence as the brightest star in his
hemisphere, he who had once had serious
thoughts of rebelling, now bowed again, an
abject slave.

During the time that Theresa was a prisoner
to the house, Mark found several opportunities
of being with his friend Bathurst, and as the
state of affairs at home was sufficient excuse

for his not accepting any invitations, he could enjoy his friend's society without the dread of being again asked to dinner.

In the course of their conversations, the late catastrophe was frequently revived, and at last Mr. Bathurst could not resist saying—

" I confess I think the loss of your ninety guinea horse served you perfectly right—why did you not trust to your own judgment rather than the word of a rogue of a horse-dealer?"

" My dear fellow, I was up to *him !*—he had very little to do either as to aiding or injuring my judgment; I was entirely biassed by my wife, who, as I told you before, had set her heart on this particular pair."

" But still, Chetwode, surely you might have represented to Mrs. Mark that the value of a horse does not consist in mere outward beauty?"

" I told her I thought the animals unsafe."

" And yet you bought them?"

" She wished it."

" She did—and by weakly (forgive me) in-

dulging a wish which I daresay one word of
yours would have changed into accordance with
your own, you endangered her life!—my good
fellow, we bachelors consider a wife much more
precious than you married men do, apparently!"

" You were not near to advise me, Bathurst."

" But even if I had been, you would not
have taken my advice."

" Yes I would—try me, prove me—what is
it for the future?"

" I *will* try you then; buy Cornwall's carriage horses and sell that showy animal you
now have—you will then have a handsome,
well-seasoned pair, and you need never be
afraid of hearing that Mrs. Mark has gone out
alone."

Mark took this advice and the horses were
bought; he had the satisfaction of his own
conscience, but he expected a grand display of
anger from the higher powers when the daring
act became known.

Contrary, however, to these anticipations,

the tidings of the new purchase were received in silence; Theresa had had a lesson and Mark was both surprised and pleased to find she had profited by it.

She even vouchsafed to admire them when they came round for the first time, and Chetwode testified his approval of such meritorious conduct by presenting her with a set of opals and emeralds, when the real truth was, the humour for opposition had passed by, and she no longer cared whether the horses had belonged to Colonel Cornwall, or had been purchased from a horsedealer.

Time wore on, and an interregnum of peace " endured for a season," but it was but for a season unfortunately.

The tranquillity was soon succeeded by constant threatenings of an irruption in the household, and even the two coachmen in the stables could not be persuaded to keep the peace.

The worst, however, was, the state of affairs

within doors, and at last they took so serious a turn that the old butler, with faltering tones, and tears in his eyes, gave warning, announcing at the same time that his equally ancient companion, the footman, would endeavour to stay, but that he feared he would find himself unable in the end;—Mr. Victor made himself so exceedingly disagreeable that there was no living with him; and now came the invidious question—who was to go, and who was to stay ?

Unhappily, on this point, Chetwode and his wife differed; the former knew how valuable to his mother were the tried and trusty domestics who had pronounced it impossible to live with the new comer, and was naturally anxious that they should be, by some means or other, induced to remain, and those means unfortunately were most repugnant to Theresa, for they were no other than the dismissal of her own servants.

"It will not remedy the evil," she argued; " you will see that even if you insist on turning Victor on the wide world and discharging a coachman in whom I have the greatest confidence; the scenes of altercation will go on just the same with new servants, for the fault lies with the old ones!—they are a very old-fashioned set, accustomed to have very much their own way, and bear a natural enmity towards one, who stands, towards them, in the objectionable light of a second mistress!"

In vain Mark endeavoured to dispel this idea, but it had taken too deep root, and Theresa refused even to listen.

"You will never convince me," said she; "I assure you I saw it from the first; none of the domestics will look upon me and my establishment as anything but interlopers, therefore if they persist in quarrelling we must just keep those who stand their ground and let the mal-contents go!"

"And thereby both annoy and inconvenience my mother!"

" My dear Mark, is *my* annoyance and inconvenience then a secondary consideration?"

" By no means, my dearest! your comfort and happiness is always my first care, but—"

" Wait—wait," said Theresa—" see what time will do; that old butler has given warning it is true, but I am sure he does not mean to go; when his clothes are all packed there will still be time enough left for us to take measures —just wait till then."

And Chetwode, as usual, acquiesced. He was indeed fairly puzzled; harassed too and vexed at the contrariety of things, he felt as if he had no heart to follow the usual routine of his daily occupations, but often sat at home, dull and dispirited, whilst Theresa was enjoying herself to the utmost of her power.

The society of his mother and sister was not likely to make Mark Chetwode much gayer, for what subjects of conversation could they have, living so completely out of the world wherewith to cheer him up?

When they had talked over the conduct of the servants, and Mrs. Bellingham's last letter —Lady Rydal's ever increasing family and Mrs. Varley's chances of becoming a Bishop's lady, their sources were run dry, and Mark, whose ear had now become too familiarised with Theresa's brilliant sketches of people and things in the large circle in which she had moved, to find any great amusement in these constant family details, thought everything " flat, stale and unprofitable" till his wife came home to rouse him from his lethargy and laugh him out of his low spirits.

Affairs had halted at this stage when suddenly, to Theresa's frantic delight, Georgina and her husband arrived in town, with the intention of taking a furnished house for two months, before settling for good at the paternal mansion in Dorsetshire.

No arrival could have happened more opportunely than this, for Theresa's temper had not been improved by the additional irritation it had received from the disputes of the servants, and a gloomy brow and silent lips were not now uncommon attendants on her presence at the dinner-table.

But with Georgy, she was all her former self—bouyant, joyous, fascinating as ever, and Georgy could not help telling Mark how much she thought her sister improved. Theresa was flattered at this opinion, but she could not return the compliment, for Georgina was looking miserably jaded and care-worn, and her smile was a very unfrequent one.

But Georgy's chief attraction, her great charm—her voice, still carried all its perfection with it, and that faultless organ still commanded the same unbounded admiration.

She had had lessons in Paris, from one of the first masters, to please her husband, and the professor had deplored, in passionate terms, her misfortune in not having been born an opera-singer, so rapidly had she improved under good tuition.

"But I am going to reward her," said Mr. Keating, one evening when he had been listening to her for nearly an hour, in breathless delight—angry even when a carriage rolling by deadened the magic sounds. "She is to have an opera-box all to herself for alternate weeks, during the two months we are in town, and I consider that she will profit by that just as much as if I gave her lessons."

"An extravagant way of teaching me," said Georgy, with a faint smile.

"That's my affair—not yours," was the reply; and Theresa's eyes struck fire, whilst to her surprise, Georgina took no notice at all of the speech.

An opera-box! Theresa repeated the words over and over to herself, and a new world seemed opening before her. Amongst all her visions of the happiness that money could procure, an opera-box had entirely escaped her, and she had never till this moment had any wish to possess one, or any idea that such an enormity of enjoyment could ever be hers; but now, as her mind dwelt more and more upon it, the wish grew stronger and stronger, and at last she suddenly exclaimed,

"Where do you mean to take this box, Francis?—what tier?—perched up in the clouds, or on the pit tier?"

"I suppose unless it is on the pit tier, Mrs. Mark, you would never enter it!—I remember of old how much easier you used to think it for young men to find you out there than higher up, so perhaps it will be the pit."

"As to young men, I have not seen one for a century, and have almost forgotten what they are like, but I hope you are not the prototype of your sex;—however, the reason I enquired was this;—I have a great mind to take the alternate weeks with you, and then, Georgy and I could enjoy it all, together."

"My dear Theresa," began Georgy, "surely you do not think I would have a box without one seat being always yours?"

" Ah, but that is not like having one of my own!—no — if you consent, the bargain is made —and you have my cheque to carry home with you—but only on the understanding that we have our alternate weeks to ourselves, and share and share alike."

" Done!" exclaimed Mr. Keating, "I will see about it the first thing to-morrow morning; but, by the bye, you have said nothing to Chetwode ?"

" There is no occasion," said Mrs. Mark carelessly, " there he is if you like to tell him, but he never interferes with my privy purse, and this is a little extravagance of my own."

The Keatings said nothing, for they neither of them liked to be the first to inform Chetwode of an arrangement of which his wife should certainly have told him herself, and on which she should undoubtedly have consulted him.

As it was, the conversation took another

turn, and in a short time the opera box was forgotten, and Mark left in ignorance.

A few days after this, it happened to be Sunday afternoon, and Chetwode was hurrying up St. James's Street on his way home, when his steps were arrested by two of his friends linked arm in arm, who insisted on stopping him. In vain he assured them he was already late—he was expected at home—he really had not a moment, for he expected people to dinner —nothing would do, for they had something very particular to say to him.

"Won't detain you a second, my dear fellow, we only want to bespeak an ivory ticket now and then—we mean to make up to you, Chetwode—don't fight shy of us, now that you have got an opera box!"

Thinking of course that they were in joke, he at first laughed it off, but finding at last that there was at all events a foundation for their pleasantry, he assured them they must have got hold of the wrong man—what had he to do with opera boxes?

"A subterfuge!" was the reply, "you cloak these luxuries under the name of Mrs. Mark then, for I swear to you I saw the plan of the house down at Sams's yesterday, and to a box on the pit tier was affixed the name of Mrs. Mark Chetwode!"

The husband went home musing. The words just spoken perfectly bewildered him, and though there seemed no chance that his friends could be mistaken, still it seemed so utterly unlikely that so public an act should have been done by his wife, entirely without his knowledge, that he could not bring himself to believe it.

The same predominant feeling, however, which always prompted him to silence on subjects which might lead to discussions, unless absolutely compelled to speak, now kept him mute during the whole of dinner, until the servants had left the room, and then he thought to himself, how could he best introduce the subject of his inward cogitations.

No one but his own family and the Keatings were present, so at last, looking up from his plate, and glancing round the table, he said—

" Do you know I have been told to-day, to my great astonishment, that 1 have an opera box this season !"

Not a word was uttered for about a minute; —we all know how long that minute seems in which every one is expected to speak, and no one does; and then Mr. Keating's *insouciant* voice broke the silence ;—

" Then you may consider yourself a lucky fellow," said he.

" It depends on the circumstances, "returned Chetwode, "for I want to know whether it be a report or a reality —I imagine Theresa is the only person who can enlighten me."

Georgina looked at her sister and coloured

crimson, wishing herself at the bottom of the sea, and feeling herself a guilty accessary, yet in point of fact so innocent.

Theresa, however, always carried off these things coolly and well, and never appeared taken by surprise, a quality which millions would give anything to possess.

"Why, it is a long story, my dear Mark: and first, as you are rather a novice, I must tell you that the opera season does not commence for a fortnight; therefore I thought there was plenty of time, some day or other, to tell you that I have agreed to go shares in a box with Georgy for two months—thus, you see, I *have* and I have *not* got an opera box—now tell me how you found it out?"

There was hardly a sentence of this speech that did not impress every one at table with the feeling that it was a most objectionable one; and the abrupt way in which her husband answered it, proved how exceedingly piqued he was.

When they went upstairs, Theresa took her sister aside, and regardless of the presence of Mrs. and Miss Chetwode, asked her to go into her own boudoir with her and "have a chat."

But to this Georgy would not agree—she had more conscience than thus to outrage good breeding, and a few minutes afterwards, when they were out of the room, she remonstrated with Theresa.

"I daresay, my dear Theresa, you did not mean it, but it would have looked so very rude!"

Theresa laughed.

"Oh, Georgy! one cannot attend to these little niceties when one is going to live one's life with people!"

"The very reason, I should say, that one ought!"

"What?—a life of acting?—that would not suit me!—but never mind that—let me tell you now all about the worries and vexations of this joint establishment."

And Theresa detailed in brief but emphatic language all the battles of constant recurrence which made existence in the old house in Hill Street almost insupportable.

When she first began her recital, Georgy thought as a matter of course, that according to the universal prophecy, her sister had already " fallen out" with her relations-in-law, and her sense of relief to find that this was not the case, was very great. Still, the united estab- lishment, even whilst peace dwelt above stairs, seemed very unlikely to hold together long, and she acknowledged that the state of things must be exceedingly disagreeable.

Whilst they were speaking, Victor entered, and gradually, with that respectful familiarity, if it may be so called, which exists amongst that class of people in other countries, he joined in the conversation with his young mistresses, and spoke feelingly upon all he had to endure for the sake of Madame.

Georgina threw oil upon the waters and tried

to impress on him the necessity of forbearance with his fellow-servants, even if they were troublesome, and then he proceeded to make himself out a very martyr, concluding by assuring Mrs. Keating, that no tranquillity, no happiness, no comfort even, could belong to that household, so long as Mr. Chetwode's establishment was united to that of his mother!

" Does he know that you are to *live* here?" asked Georgy with some surprise when he was gone. " Have you ever explained to him that it is your *home*?"

" No—it was no affair of his;" answered Theresa, " if the old lady had interfered with me in any way, or the young one either, I would not have made it my home, for you know we are only trying how we like it."

From all that Theresa said, from all that fell from Mark, and from their own silent observations the Keatings very soon saw that the union of the two families could not by any possibility last much longer, and they often made the uncomfortable understanding which appeared to exist between the husband and wife, the subject of grieved and melancholy conversation between them.

That Chetwode was unhappy was evident; that he was completely under the dominion of his wife was also apparent; and Mr. Keating never uttered a greater truism than when, with his usual abruptness, he one day exclaimed—

" If Chetwode had not been, and were not still, so blindly devoted to Theresa as to imagine her faultless in spite of his own eyes and his own judgment, he would be in as fair a way to cut his throat as any man I know."

And truly Mark Chetwode was altered!— every line in his countenance—those tell-tale lines drawn by the finger of secret grief or repining—told that his life was not happy, and they seemed to deepen every day; every one saw it except she who should have been the first, and she pursued her gay and careless career day by day, night after night, bought new dresses and framed new fancies, regardless of his feelings, and unconscious of his altered looks!

Young, beautiful, admired and charmed with admiration, there was no steady affection at the bottom of that gay and selfish heart to attach her either to her husband, or her home. Theresa only looked for enjoyment beyond its limits; she did not appear aware that it was possible to be gay or even cheerful by her own fireside, and here again the weak submission of Mark Chetwode tended only to spoil her still more, for when he saw her happy and gay, there was a spell upon him so that he could not reprove.

In the case of the Opera-box he was more hurt and piqued than offended, but he said little; that little met the same scornful retorts now so familiar to his ear and so he let her take her own way, in dumb disapproval.

It is very doubtful whether Theresa even ob- served this;—as long as she was amused, she

did not pay much attention to how people
looked, and if tones distateful to her ear were
employed, she took measures effectually to
silence them.

So passed some weeks, till one by one,
nearly all the old servants of Hill-street had
signified their intention of looking out for other
houses, and at last Mrs. Chetwode, with a
faltering voice and tearful eyes, took courage
to speak to her son.

She confessed to him that much of her comfort depended on those who had so long served
her, and admitted that she could not without
the greatest reluctance consent to their leaving
her, merely because the three comparative
strangers who had joined their number, made
them miserable.

She gently suggested that the whole case
should be carefully examined, and those who
appeared not in fault whether old or new, dismissed; but not that three should retain both
place and power to the expulsion of all the rest.

In mournful earnestness Mark talked the matter over and over again, and at last agreed that the proposed plan should be submitted to Theresa, begging that his mother would take it upon herself to do so, because he knew that he could not be firm enough himself.

Poor Mrs. Chetwode's worst quality was her yielding nature, and Mark in this, was her very own child, so, between the two, the result of a conference so awkward and so difficult, may be easily guessed.

The haughty displeasure of Theresa, when the subject was carefully explained to her, was checked by none of the delicate regard for private feelings which tinctured every word uttered by her mother-in-law; she made no scruple of using language which sank deeply into the old lady's heart, and ended, by announcing her determination not to part with either Victor, or her own maid.

In vain Mrs. Chetwode put the case in every point of view—in vain she represented the many long years spent by each trusty domestic in that once peaceful house ; nothing would do.

" You, naturally, stand by *your* servants," was Theresa's reply, " and I stand by mine ; you say you cannot possibly part with yours and I do not see why mine should not be equally essential to *my* comfort; thus I see but one plan—"

" My dear, you have only to name it," said Mrs. Chetwode, " and I will do my utmost to further it."

But she little dreamt what this plan was : she little dreamt that rather than sacrifice a little personal inconvenience, Theresa proposed dividing the two establishments from top to bottom, and separating the mother and her son—leaving the house that he had so fondly hoped would be their home, and taking another roof to shelter them, within the limits too, of the same quarter, of the same metropolis !

No words can describe the dismay, the

pained astonishment, and the absolute grief of Mrs. Chetwode, when first, in words as void of all emotion as though she were talking on the most agreeable subject in the world, Theresa suggested this arrangement.

Fraught with a bitterness incomprehensible to herself, it met no sanction, no encouragement, no tolerance even ; but the mother little knew with whom she had to deal ! The idea had sprung to life in a brain as resolute as it was active, and in spite of entreaties which almost took the form of prayers, Theresa adhered to her opinion, that it was the best and the only plan, of all that ingenuity could devise, for future peace and future comfort.

So secure was she of gaining the day, so confident was she now, of her influence over her husband, that she no longer, as hitherto, endeavoured to waylay him on his return home, and so possess herself of that power which they say clings to the " first word;" she knew her ground perfectly, and in her own mind, every sentence

o 2

was ready for him. Mark had but to come home, to listen and to agree, and a plan which had long smouldered in her breast, would wake to life and be put in force, in spite of his mother —in spite of himself.

It is a common old saying, that the more we have, the more we want; and for some time past, Theresa had found the possession of a carriage of her own, so far preferable to driving about in those of other people, that she naturally inferred, that a house of her own would be much more agreeable, than being nobody but the son's wife, in that of a mother-in-law.

The march of pride did not stop here; she had very often, on the occasion of dinner-parties, felt inwardly annoyed that her husband should be at the head of the table, and herself sit at the side; she felt it a great grievance, and thought that Mrs. Chetwode should have resigned the seat of honour to her, from the first, little thinking, that the old lady had fought a hard battle with her son, to induce him to allow her so to do, a measure which he, from the earliest date of their arrangements, vehemently opposed.

In short, everything now seemed to have been a conspiracy for no inconsiderable time, towards the desired consummation; and Theresa thought the present so excellent an opportunity for dissolving the partnership, that she resolved not to let it slip.

Consequently, on Mark's return that evening, she called him to her room, and after completely wearying his ear with new grievances and the recital of new disputes, she asked him what on earth they were to do, for to go on in this way, was misery to him, to his mother, to herself, and to every one concerned.

Chetwode quite agreed to this; no one could be more sensible than himself that it was so, yet he shrank from hazarding the only remedy that occurred to him, meaning, the discharge of his own servants.

Theresa saw that he was too straightforward to understand her hints, and that if she wished to be understood, she must speak out at once; therefore doubtingly, ambiguously, and in rather a nervous voice, she disclosed her plan.

It was very, very long after that day, before Theresa forgot the look and the movement with which her husband received the confession from her lips, that she thought there would be no peace *until they had a home of their own.*

Unfortunately, Theresa's was not a simple, honest nature; unfortunately, she had once or twice deceived her husband, and more than once or twice acted with a double motive, as he had afterwards discovered; consequently, when first the light burst upon him, and her desire to leave his mother's roof was not to be mistaken, the thought instantly struck him that during his absence that day, something must have occurred to have inspired her with the sudden wish—something too terrible for him to frame in words—possibly, a family quarrel!

To him, the shock that her suggestion gave him was like a stroke of lightning, for it came upon him without the smallest preparation, and that, combined with the idea that entered his mind almost at the same moment, so completely overpowered him, that he started upright from the chair in which he had listlessly thrown himself, and fixed on Theresa the look which had so alarmed her.

She was acute enough, however, partly to interpret his thoughts, and thereby to relieve his mind of part of its load, without any unnecessary delay, and certainly that relief tended in a measure to calm his agitation; but the shock had been too great, for him to give any decided reply. He required to think about it—to weigh it on all sides—to see if he could ever make up his mind to leave that house, and deliberately to judge whether there were actually no altérnative to so painful, so unexpected, a step.

Here again, Theresa's tact did a great deal. Contrary to her usual custom, she did not attempt to " talk him down," but gave him time to think; it was days even, before the subject was again renewed, or even touched upon, and at the end of that period, she had her reward, she gained her point—and the triumph of hearing him say, that after mature consideration, the step she had suggested appeared to him both wise and unavoidable, was hers.

After the decision was made and announced, the worst seemed over, and yet Mark's spirits did not rally.

Whilst brooding over the remarks which people might make, and shrinking with all the horror of a sensitive nature, from the many mis-interpretations which might be put upon the fact of the double establishment not having answered, his aunt Bellingham's prophetic voice rang again in his ears.

" Mark my words—it *will not* answer!" And here, in three months, those words had indeed come true.

There are no trials, however, in human nature, which do not, after a time, become familiarised to our feelings, although at first they may have appeared too painful to contemplate.

Chetwode, by degrees, grew resigned, though not reconciled, to the change about to take place, and then the only part of it, which he could not get over at all, was, removing to another house in London. Had his future home been in the back woods of America, it seemed to him as though it would have been preferable ; for then the world would have no room to say that his wife and his mother were unable to live happily together—and Chetwode was beginning now to be morbidly alive as to what " the world " thought and said.

To Theresa, this sentiment was incompre-

hensible, but Georgy entered into it immediately, she so sympathised in the sadness
of her good and excellent brother-in-law, that
at last he took to going to her house of a
morning, and sitting over her fire by the hour
together, lost in thought.

It was after a long reverie of this kind one
day, that, on his suddenly exclaiming—

" If I had but any fair excuse for going
abroad again, or anywhere in the world but
London !"………

Georgina cheerfully answered—

‘ Why not think of the country?—why not
take a house for the summer months in some
nice county, and there sit quietly down, and
resolve your future plans!"

Mark was struck with the idea, and seemed
suddenly animated into life again—

" Upon my word, Georgy, no bad idea!—
but then—Theresa!"

" Theresa would like it—she often said so."

" But what county?—I never thought of that till now—I have hardly a country acquaintance."

" You forget Francis Keating and his wife," said Georgy with a smile, and seeing that the spark had caught, with her usual good taste, she said no more.

CHAPTER XI.

AND now, the time came round for Mrs. Bellingham to arrive in town for her six months of London life, and the moment she became aware of how matters stood in Hill Street, she marched off thither in a state of such delight at the verifying of her prophecy, that one would have thought Rochefoucauld had written his bitter truism about the " misfortunes of one's friends" expressly for her.

This delight was of course in a measure

damped, when she learnt, and saw, that it was no incompatibility of temper between the young and the old mistress of the Hill Street house, that had caused the revolution; but there was considerable satisfaction in the idea that Victor was at the bottom of it.

Victor had always been odious in her sight, and she now hoped Mark had had enough of him, for of course, after his valorous deeds in thus disorganizing a household, to gain an end decidedly beneficial to himself, her nephew was not going to keep him?

And then Mark had to say, that he was; that Victor was a valuable and useful servant, and—most conclusive of all reasons—Theresa wished him to stay.

"Then mark my words—they have come true more than once—*you'll repent it*," said the old lady, with a world of meaning in her eyes, and he was very much provoked at her, for experience had rather made him dread a prophecy of Mrs. Bellingham's.

"That impertinent old woman!" exclaimed
Theresa to her sister one morning—"if you
only knew how very difficult it is, to sit and
listen with any patience to all her inquisitive
questions!—just as if she had any right to
enquire into Mark's affairs now, as she
did when he was a bachelor! and to interfere
with our servants too!—she is a female Bathurst, Georgy, only Mr. Bathurst does it all
underground—*he* works in the dark, and the
effects come out in daylight!—Ah, Georgy,
you little know, you, with your calm happy life
what it is to be torn to pieces by one's relations-in-law!"

Georgy said nothing, but she sighed.

"You never seem to me to have any worries, or else they are not begun," continued
Theresa.

"There is a skeleton in every cupboard,"
quoted her sister, "and you must not expect
to have everything smooth; for my part, your

lot seems to me singularly happy, for you have the best of husbands"...

"Oh, yes—a very good man in his way only as obstinate as a mule, begging his pardon; it is the daily task of my life to learn how to manage him."

"I should have thought the lesson learnt," laughed Georgy.

"No—not as long as Mr. Bathurst's influence, and Mrs. Bellingham's presence, lead him out of the right path; now you cannot complain of *this*, Georgy!"

"No—I complain of nothing — I never should, Theresa, if I had ever so much cause, for in all marriages it strikes me that it is ten to one against *us!*—if I had a daughter I should teach her this, that more than half of the happiness of married life, depends upon *us* —whatever faults your husband has, shut your eyes, for you will never, never cure them!"

"Trust *me!*" cried Theresa, clenching her hand, half in joke, and half in earnest—"only let me discover any really serious fault in *my* husband, and you should soon see if I could not discover a way to cure it too."

This conversation passed from Theresa's memory like "the breath-stain on glass," till some days afterwards, when, Mrs. Bellingham happening to be at dinner in Hill Street, the subject of the society they had moved in in Paris was being discussed, and she remarked that during the many years that she had wintered in Paris, she had never known so many pretty women assembled together, before.

After enumerating them one by one, Madame D'Esterville's name was mentioned—

"Surely you do not call *her* pretty!" cried Theresa, whose organ of veneration was very slightly developed, and who had not the least regard or respect for Mrs. Bellingham, "you cannot admire *her*, I hope!—if you do, I am astonished at your taste."

Nothing annoys people so much as sayin "I am surprised at your taste," or, "I thought you had better taste," for it is a polite way of telling them how very inferior you think them, or how much they have sunk in your estimation since you discovered their peculiar objects of admiration.

"I consider her *very* pretty," returned Mrs. Bellingham testily, "and very good style; she is in the best society; I think, Mrs. Mark, you met her at my house."

"Did I?—yes, I daresay I did, but I don't remember; I only know I met her very often when we were all girls."

"I knew nothing of her before her marriage; she married well, and then I became acquainted with her, as she moved in my set then."

"Did she?—ah; but you know *we* were everywhere; we were not limited to a narrow circle—however we never could endure Annie Manners, and of course we did not change our opinion when she became Madame d'Esterville, for in *our* wide set, we liked pleasant people, and poor stupid grandees we thought nothing at all of!"

It was such speeches as these, speeches cutting every way, which made Mark feel as though he were sitting on thorns, and vexed him to such a degree that he could hardly endure to remain in the room, but to Mrs. Bellingham, they were rather acceptable than otherwise, for it gave her an opportunity which she rarely enjoyed, of exchanging sarcasms with one, well able to compete with her, and whose own brilliant sallies of contemptuous bitterness, had only the effect of drawing out her own powers.

" I cannot of course form any opinion," said Mrs. Bellingham in the calmest of voices, " as to the style of beauty, or even the sort of person likely to captivate the taste of yourself and Mrs. Dering, because, naturally, everyone measures their standard of perfection according to the sphere in which they move,and the station in life they occupy! I can only speak on my own authority, and I can only name one mutual friend who *particularly* admired, Madame D'Esterville—your brother-in-law Mr. Keating."

Theresa coloured crimson—she well knew of the admiration, so foolishly published, which Francis Keating entertained for the pretty coquette in question, and she well knew also, the frequent heart-aches, to her sister, of which it had been the cause—but these mortifying facts, she fancied were locked in their own bosoms, and though Mrs. Bellingham's words were home-strokes which Theresa could not deny were well-deserved, still she was not one to allow them to pass without their answer.

" My brother-in-law admired Annie *Manners*," said she, haughtily and pointedly, " and flirted with her too, but you are mistaken in supposing and in saying, that he is the least inclined to carry on the amusement with Madame D'Esterville ;—he was nearly as intimate at her mother's house as we were, and know, as well as we do, what a puppet, what a doll, she was!—but perhaps in the society in which she now moves, these defects pass unobserved."

"I yield to your superior authority," returned Mrs. Bellingham, "and can only plead for excuse, the poor evidence of my own eyes; if they were mistaken, believe me it would give me great satisfaction, considering that I look upon Mrs. Keating as one of the most attractive young women I know."

Mrs. Chetwode rose from the table the instant there was a pause, because she thought the dialogue was becoming too severe, but though the conversation was thus broken off, Theresa mused upon it in her lounging chair after dinner, and recalled every word of it.

How completely did Mrs. Bellingham possess the power of insinuating, in a few words, things which might make material for many and many an hour of uneasy reflection! Theresa had provoked her, and therefore she had exerted this power, otherwise perhaps, for the sake of her nephew, she might have been more guarded and less bitter.

Yet as far as facts were concerned, she had not advanced a word more than the truth; people who study to be universal favorites, and to please everybody, never speak the " plain truth;" there is a great prejudice in general, against speaking it; and when we have a friend whom we think would benefit by having it told him, we get an enemy who has a soft tongue and a smooth manner, and whose reputation of friendship cannot be injured thereby, to do " the dirty work " in our stead.

But Mrs. Bellingham liked to do this herself; she entrusted to no one the happiness and triumph, of dethroning upstarts from their self-elected eminence, and saying to a *parvenu* " Friend, come down lower."

Theresa carried herself too high; she had forgotten too soon, that the place and power which she enjoyed, and the position she held, were entirely owing to the agency of her husband, and Mrs. Bellingham seeing this, lost no opportunity, however remote from the grievance of the moment, of pulling her down from her pedestal.

She could not have done this more effectually, than by the means she had on this evening adopted, for the insinuations she had thrown out revived in Theresa's mind her late conversation with her sister, and made her think to herself,

" If this old woman is speaking the truth, perhaps every word that poor Georgy uttered to me had some point in it, and every sigh, some meaning."

And then she recollected how emphatically she had spoken of married life and its trials, and also her sad but significant quotation—

" There is a skeleton in every cupboard !"

Her altered looks too, spoke volumes; there must have been some cause for them, and when Theresa thought, and thought, till she became certain that Georgy was tortured by her husband's frivolity and thoughtlessness, her anger turned from Mrs. Bellingham, and settled upon her brother-in-law instead.

This then, was Georgina's ' skeleton in the cupboard!' just as Mark Chetwode's weakness and obstinacy was hers !! and Theresa felt infinitely more indignant against her sister's husband, than she did even against her own !

A few nights after this, when the sisters were at the Opera together, and Mr. Keating had absented himself nearly the whole evening, Theresa, who determined to find out whether he kept up his old habits, or whether Mrs. Bellingham's insinuations were without foundation, asked Georgy plainly, where he was?

She said she did not know, but supposed, in some friend's box, " for," she added, trying to laugh, " Francis would think it very old-fashioned to be seen with his wife and sister-in-law, when he has a seat at his service in several other parts of the house."

" Then he does not come entirely for the music, as he boasts," said Theresa, " he cannot quite give up his ancient love of flirting."

" Oh it is not his fault!" exclaimed Georgy almost petulantly, " women are so foolish, Theresa!—really if you had but seen as much of the conduct of pretty young married women as I have lately, you would not wonder that husbands are sometimes led away ; I never say anything, because it only makes matters worse, but I am very certain——"

" Of what?" asked Theresa as her sister paused.

" I will not finish my sentence—I was going to be ill-natured; all I will say is, that women turn men's heads sadly."

It was not often the sisters were left alone even for a few moments, and Theresa was just going to take advantage of this opportunity of putting some leading questions, when there was a knock at the door.— Georgy rose and opened it. It was the box-keeper with a note for Mr. Keating, and she took it from him, saying that she would give it to him when he returned which would, be very shortly.

" A note ?" cried Theresa, all on the *qui vive*, and charmed at the mystery of it, for the box-keeper had hesitated, and was disinclined to give it up, had not Georgy taken it out of his hand, " a note for Francis! sealed too—pink, and pink wax, and some detestable scent I declare—whose hand-writing is it, Georgy ?"

Georgy had no idea; the space for the address was so small, from the note being twisted into the shape of a knot, that the hand was necessarily cramped, and therefore irrecognisable.

" Is there not a scrap to be seen?—not a letter or a line, *anyhow* ?" persisted Mrs. Mark Chetwode, dying to get it into her possession.

" For shame," said Georgy gravely, " what is it to us? I have not even looked at the seal Theresa, so do not expect me to try and gratify your curiosity."

Soon after this, different gentlemen joined them, and at last, Keating himself returned.

Theresa saw Georgina place the note quietly in his hands, so quietly that the action attracted no notice and he glanced over it at the back of the box and thrust it into his pocket, without a syllable of explanation.

Theresa quite panted with indignation. " Oh you poor, tame, excellent wife!" thought she. " I only wish it had been *my* husband, and no power on earth should have prevented my exposing him, and making his face tingle for very shame!—Georgy! Georgy! how you spoil that man!"

And soon after Keating abruptly left the box. Another visitor left at the same time, and Sir Henry Wharton alone remained. It was getting late; the ballet was drawing to a close, and a few had already dropt off, when suddenly Theresa exclaimed that she was tired to death, that she felt quite faint, she would give worlds to go, and if Georgy would not be angry, would she allow Sir Henry to look for the carriage.

" But Francis?" said Georgy, anxiously.

" I don't want *you* to go," said Theresa; " I can go home by myself, and send it back for you; only I feel as if I should faint—so if Sir Henry would but be so kind—"

He was ready, as usual, to do anything he was asked: but he nevertheless tried to prevail on her to sit till the end, " because she always did," but finding persuasion of no avail, he departed on his errand.

No sooner had the door closed on him, than Theresa sprang from her seat, with a bound which terrified Georgy into an idea that she had gone suddenly mad, she gained the back of the box, and seizing something from the ground, held it up in triumph.

There, in her upraised hand, was the pink note, crushed, and screwed almost into two pieces—but there it was.

" Thank me for my *ruse*," she cried; " thank

me for not exposing Francis by exhibiting his *billet-doux* before Sir Henry; but ask of me no forbearance—do not suppose that I am not going to read it, now that I have got it—not a word, Georgina, *for I am determined.*"

Georgina sat stricken by a thousand contending feelings; deadly pale, and trembling with the dread of her husband's inopportune return at such a moment, she could only stammer out,

" Theresa, I entreat you—I implore you not; —the meanness—the dishonour. Theresa, in mercy—for my sake, do not read it."

" I will;—I have—" exclaimed her sister, still greedily examining her treasure. " I am resolved to find it all out for you."

" But I do not wish to know," cried Georgy.

" Then *I do,*" said Theresa; " and I will read it to you. You cannot help my reading it to you, and it is no fault of yours if I choose to do so; leave it all in my hands, and you shall not be blamed—but only listen:—"

"'I have this moment heard you have an opera-box, and have secured a seat with the Baroness for this evening. Find your way to No. XIII., as I have volumes to say to you.'

"And here, in one corner," continued Theresa, " are the initials, ' A. D'E.,' so pray what do you think of that?"

" Nothing," returned Georgy with a violent effort at self-command, yet her voice changed and trembled, in spite of herself; " nothing at all—only I had no idea she was in town even. Give me the note, Theresa."

But Theresa would not; she was determined to keep so precious a weapon in her own hands, and insisted on Georgy saying nothing at all about it; she would restore it to her brother-in-law herself, and begged her sister to rest assured she should not spare him, when she once began to tell him he was found out.

Of this, Georgina had not the smallest doubt,

but it was painful to her, beyond words, to think that Francis was to smart under the lash of so violent a temper as that of Theresa; it might make a breach between them for ever, and worse than all, undermine her own bright plots and plans for fixing her sister close to her in the country. If Francis once took offence, his nature was not forgiving, and it was very unlikely but that the discovery just made, would annoy and irritate him exceedingly.

"And after all," said Georgy, "it may not be his fault; if she will write him notes, and tempt him away, and turn his head, it is not his fault."

"No," answered Theresa; "not in the least —only a little failing on his part. But be that as it may, he married my sister, and Annie D'Esterville shall never write to him again if *I* can help it."

When Sir Henry Wharton returned to say that the carriage was ready and waiting, Theresa was quite recovered, and wished to stay to the last, whilst Georgy, heart-sick and uneasy, would gladly have gone home.

Thinking, however, that perhaps her husband would be annoyed if she did so, contrary to her usual custom, she did not contest the point, but remained till Mr. Keating came to fetch them, and put her arm within his, as calmly as though nothing at all had occurred.

The next day, prompt, energetic, and still just as warm on her subject as she had been the evening before, Theresa drove down to the Travellers the moment she entered the carriage and sending in for Mr. Keating, told him to get in, for she had something to say to him.

The forbearance of her sister had only had the effect of rousing her to still greater anger —not, perhaps, all directed against himself; more than half being against the designing girl who had been their rival in their gay maiden days, and whose present passion for flirting,

accordingly appeared all the more repre-
hensible.

" A piece of your property has fallen into
my hands," were her first words.   " Think over
the last few days, and recollect what you have
lost."

He could recollect nothing, and when, after
much time spent in artful cross-questioning,
she produced the pink note and held it before
his eyes, he received it with a burst of laughter.

Neither duped nor pacified, Theresa pursued
her point, and to his laughing replies, gave him
back as much vehement impertinence as he
could well put up with; but in the end she
gained the advantage, as she thought, for he
asked her to let the matter rest where it was,
and not worry Georgy by telling her anything
about it.

" For I give you my honour," he added,
" that is the first note I ever had from her, and

I do not believe she means any harm; she is an amusing little woman, and as you well know not very wise, so do not turn a trifle into a serious charge, but give me the note and forget all about it."

"I shall not easily forget it," retorted Theresa; "though you may have your note back. As to your honour, do not trouble yourself to stake that, for I consider a married man as much bound by honour to study appearances, as he is to regulate his conduct—and appearances are exceedingly against you."

"You are jealous of Madame D'Esterville," laughed Mr. Keating; "and so is Georgy."

"Georgy!" repeated the sister, indignantly, "Georgy behaved beautifully—as *even you* must acknowledge. Thank your stars *I* was not your wife, or this would not have passed so quietly."

"I do thank my stars—cordially. All I want to impress on you is, the folly of making mountains of mole-hills in this life. Madame

D'Esterville arrived in England that very day, and knowing that Georgy disliked her exceedingly, yet not wishing entirely to cut our acquaintance——"

" She writes a confidential *billet-doux* to my sister's husband, which he receives as mysteriously as it was sent," interrupted Theresa. " yes, yes, I know ; all very harmless on your part, and very innocent on hers! Annie D'Esterville was always so artless and inexperienced ; but depend upon it, whilst I have the distinguished honor and privilege of her acquaintance, she shall know that the happiness of my sister is not to be endangered by any aid or influence of hers !"

" Georgy's happiness rests I trust on a firmer foundation," said Mr. Keating gravely. " I charge you, Theresa, as seriously as I caution you, not to be intemperate, or you may do mischief."

Theresa repeated the conversation to her sister and Georgina was tranquillised by it ;

she said it was exactly what she had expected ; that the blame was Madame D'Esterville's, whose nature was vain, frivolous and intriguing, but that Francis was too honorable to say so ; if she chuse to flatter and follow him for the sake of securing a *cavalier* with whom she had once had such successful flirtations, it was not likely that he would resist the amusement of talking nonsense with so pretty a woman.

" Do not judge him harshly, Theresa," said she in conclusion, " for you cannot have had any experience in a case like this ; Mr. Chetwode is not the man to make you jealous, and when Francis grieves and vexes me I know he does not mean it, although I confess it is very hard to bear."

Mark was greatly pleased at the part Theresa had taken in this affair when it came to his knowledge, for it raised Theresa in his estimation, and he was gratified to see she possessed so much and such keen feeling on the only point in her character in which he had once fancied she might be a little deficient.

She who had so vehemently resented on the part of her sister, a husband's neglect, would, he thought, be the best judge in the world of that pure and simple line of conduct which best became a wife, and thus his admiration and his confidence were now greater than ever.

But the episode did not end here. A few nights after this, the Chetwodes were at a ball, and as they entered the room the first couple Theresa saw, were Monsieur and Madame D'Esterville, standing in the midst of the circle.

Theresa immediately went up to them, and addressed M. D'Esterville in French. He was a stiff, starched, exceedingly dignified man, who had the reputation of being one of the most strict and severe of husbands.

Whilst she was speaking, she heard Madame D'Esterville ask Mark, if Mrs. Keating were there that night, so, turning suddenly towards her, and still speaking in French, in order that her husband might have the full benefit, she said—

" No—nor Mr. Keating either; he was not with us the other night, when you sent him that note, asking him to come to your box; I hope you found some other *preux chevalier* to fill his place."

The colour of Madame D'Esterville's cheeks and the lighting up of her husband's eyes were delicious to Theresa, and she passed on, satisfied that her task was done, and her animosity appeased, for it was now amply sated.

Mark was sorry the speech had been made; he told his wife so directly, and rather wondered at the cool effrontery with which she had delivered it.

" It paid off many an old score!" said Theresa.

" To little purpose," replied Chetwode— " the very fact of your being aware of her having written that note to Keating, will be her best defence; she will say there was no harm in an act not clandestinely committed."

" No excuse in the eyes of Monsieur

D'Esterville," interrupted Theresa; "for I know him too well; she must take very good care if ever she wishes to send another note to a gentleman, so my object is attained."

In this case, whilst Theresa thought she had manfully fought her sister's battle, she had in fact only satisfied the cravings of personal pique. Georgy was vexed with her, and as far as Mr. Keating was concerned, she had not struck at the root of the evil; she had but lopped off a branch, and that only by accident, for as long as he existed, he must have had some one to flirt with, it being his nature, and as circumstances took the D'Estervilles from Town a few days after this, he immediately looked out for some one else to fill her vacant place.

But throughout all this, Georgina never complained : her husband's temper was variable, and at times excessively passionate, but never did those calm lips utter one word of retort, or those mild eyes look one glance of reproach.

He was a tiresome being to deal with; but

never was the patience of his wife worn out, or her placidity disturbed.

Well might Mrs. Dering once have said, " I defy you to ruffle my Georgy !" for certainly, after the trials Mr. Keating often put her to, it did seem quite impossible.

There she sat hour after hour at the piano, sometimes practising a song to please him till she was hoarse with repetition; at others, going over and over again the same passage of some difficult accompaniment, and all the time subject to his vehement expressions of wrath, and intemperate bursts of impatience, but answering nothing, and steadily refraining, by word, look, and deed, from adding to his irritation.

" I could not, I would not, be the slave you are !" cried Theresa, one day; " we certainly were penniless girls, with nothing to make our husbands grateful to us for marrying them, but as to indulging a man in the way you do your husband, I would see all the husbands in the world at the bottom of the sea first."

" We swore at the altar," said Georgy, simply and laconically.

" Yes, to love, honor and obey, but not to be treated badly—and yet, Georgy, I often think to myself in spite of Francis's temper you really are very happy, after your own fashion ?"

" The heart knoweth its own bitterness," murmured Georgina, but the murmur was so low that it did not reach Theresa's ears, and fortunate that it was so, for a moment after, she wished the repining words unsaid.

DURING the last few weeks of gaiety and excitement, peace had dwelt in the house in Hill Street, and the old servants had even allowed their month of probation to pass, without taking any notice, so smoothly had the days fleeted by.

But in spite of this, Mark did not venture to hope that this state of things would last for ever; he felt that the flames were only smouldering, and that a spark at any moment was sufficient to set it all in a blaze again; consequently, the careless words once dropped by Georgy as to his trying what a few months absence in the country would effect, now recurred still more forcibly to his memory, and he and Theresa began seriously to consider whether it would not be their wisest plan.

As for Theresa, the project was new, and so, was sure to find favour in her sight; besides which, she had no ties to attach her to London when Georgy was gone, therefore they were amongst the happiest moments of Mark Chetwode's life in which he sat shut up with Theresa for hours in her boudoir, talking over a subject on which for a wonder they thought in unison, and arranging plans for a future to which they both looked forward with delight.

To Mrs. Bellingham, their proposition of attempting a country life, appeared in the light of a wild-goose scheme, for though, out of kindness to Mrs. Chetwode, they said they were only to try it for a few months, she saw that if they met with any very tempting residence, they were both keen enough on the subject just then, to hamper themselves, perhaps for some time.

Consequently she felt it her duty to offer due opposition, and as usual since her nephew's marriage, her veto met nothing but indifference, for Theresa only permitted him to listen, and not to argue the point with her.

The next consideration, after having mutually agreed that they were ready to leave Town, was, where should they go?—They leant most, very naturally, towards Dorsetshire, as being Georgina's county, indeed they knew no other.

Mrs. Chetwode had a great fancy for Kent; poor, good soul, she knew it was called the Garden of England and she had been for many summers domiciled for a few months at Tunbridge Wells, therefore the beauty of Frant, Speldhurst, Bayham and Penshurst, had convinced her that no spot on earth could boast of such scenery; but she did not consider that when people look for a home in a county of England they must not imagine scenery alone will constitute the happiness of a country life; people cannot live without society—at least, not unless they wish to grow rusty from inaction whilst the wheels of the world around them are whirling their ceaseless course of business and pleasure;—and to hope to enter into the society of a strange county without a few good introductions, if not of a herald to trumpet one's fame, is absurd.

Where then could the Chetwodes expect a better reception in than that part of the county where Georgina was to live, for besides the large circle who would wish to become acquainted with Theresa for the sake of her sister, was there not also Ringmere within twelve miles, the seat of Lord Rydal?

When this occurred to Mrs. Bellingham her objections were in a manner cancelled and she acknowledged that to her daughter Rydal, the acquaintance of Theresa would be a pleasure and an advantage, as there were few young people in her neighbourhood with whom she could associate; therefore perhaps on the whole she might not be quite justified in withholding her sanction.

The question of the county being settled, it now only remained for them to consider how they should set about looking for a house, and Georgina was asked to dinner on purpose to be consulted.

When she and her husband arrived, they were prepared with the very best plan in the world, and that was, that Mr. Chetwode and Theresa should accompany them down to their home at Major Keating's, and remain guests there, until they had seen every available place in the neighbourhood.

" There are one or two to be let within seven miles of us," said Georgy; " and one to be sold; the loveliest spot you ever saw, only they ask too much, and the house has stood empty for many years; you remember on the

high road, Theresa, just outside the Keating
grounds!—you remember the green lane
parellel with the river?—the lodge gate of
Seaton opens into that lane, and the avenue of
magnificent chesnut trees is nearly half a mile
long; how I do hope Mr. Chetwode may be
tempted!"

Georgy need not have said to her sister,
" do you remember?"—for well, too well she
remembered all the lovely lanes, and walks, and
drives, round that favoured spot;—the question
carried her rapidly back to those happy, dreamy
days, when life seemed too bright, and the hours
far too short—when for a brief space her heart
took sovereignty over her colder nature, and
she was a girl, loving and beloved, instead of
a worldly, artificial woman.

And immediately in her breast there sprang
up an intense wish to see those scenes again;
to be once more wandering in those well known
lanes, and sitting on the red banks of that
silvery river, so the invitation was gladly and

cordially accepted, and they were to follow the Keatings into Dorsetshire, after allowing them a week or ten days to settle in Georgina's new home.

Yet it made Theresa melancholy to think over those days, and she wondered what she should feel when she visited the hallowed haunts again.

A name, that had never since her marriage been uttered by her, hovered on her lips, but she refrained from breathing it; that name, so intimately connected with the scenes to which she was about to return, hung upon every sentence, but she dare not speak it!

And yet she had hitherto always taught herself to think, that he who bore it was forgotten.

Once only, when she and Georgy were one evening sitting alone, her reserve forsook her for a moment, and the subject was faintly approached; Georgy was saying how enchanting it would be if Mr. Chetwode should take a great fancy to Seaton, and purchase it at once.

"I am not sure," was Theresa's rejoinder, "I cannot help thinking that seeing all those old haunts again will be very painful... to *me*."

"Oh no—no!" exclaimed Georgy hastily—"not that, dear Theresa; I hope all that has quite gone by."

No more was said, for both felt that each had been understood, but the impression left on Georgina's mind was an uncomfortable one; she had so often in secret trusted and prayed that Theresa's volatile mind had indeed forgotten, yet those few words of deep meaning proved that she had *not!*

When the Keatings left town, there were four or five nights of the opera box left to Theresa's share, and Chetwode asked her one morning, if she would not invite a few of their mutual friends to enjoy the benefit of a treat, not often placed within reach of plodding young barristers.

Theresa was not very well pleased at this request; she considered it a suggestion that infringed upon her own rights, and she said that if there was anything in the world she hated, it was, exhibiting people whom she did not consider " presentable" in the box !

During the whole two months that the sisters had shared their luxury, Chetwode might have reminded his wife, that never once had any friend of his, been honoured with a ticket, but he refrained, for he hoped that it had been unintentional on her part; now, however, it appeared that it had not been so, and he tried to impress on her the fact, that even his Aunt Bellingham had not been paid the common civility of being invited.

"Because I never will be seen with three ladies," was Theresa's answer—"it looks so detestable to see every chair in a box occupied —I had rather not go at all; than that."

"You would not have had three," returned Mark, " my aunt does not consider Mary

Vere her shadow by any means; and really, my dear Theresa, considering the intimate terms of friendship on which Bathurst and I have always lived, he must think my present neglect of him very strange."

"I cannot help what he thinks; but does that mean that I am to invite him too?"

"Does that mean?" was a phrase peculiarly displeasing to Mark, but what could he say? what could he do?—except put up with it.

"If his company is not actually disagreeable to you, it would really oblige me if you paid him this little attention."

Theresa was silent, but the pinched look about her lips told, that it was anything but agreeable.

"Any one else?" said she at last, as handing her husband a note for Mrs. Bellingham, she asked if that would do.

"No," answered Chetwode, "I know you do not like your number to exceed four, so

with your permission I will make the fourth—
for to-morrow, is it not ?"

As it happened, Mr. Bathurst was engaged,
but in his free and easy style, wrote back, that
any other night would suit him equally well.

Mrs. Bellingham accepted, and was rather
pleased with the civility—we are always gratified when people we dislike, or who give themselves airs to us, pay us some unexpected attention—and thus Theresa was fairly " hampered"
as she called it, for two nights instead of one!

However, the bustle and excitement of the
last week in town, reconciled her in a measure
to the infliction, and Mrs. Bellingham made
herself so agreeable, that Theresa resolved, that
on Mr. Bathurst's night, she would ask for her
company again.

Mrs. Mark could not have a better companion,
in the mysterious gloom of an opera-box in the
olden time of dark red draperies, than Mrs.
Bellingham, for she seemed to take but little

heed of the various visitors who came to pay their respects to the beautiful young wife.

She had her 'best eye,' as we have already observed, and before she had been an hour in the box, Theresa placed her, so that its powers were restricted more to the exterior, than the interior, and that, not because any one of the butterflies who fluttered in and out, had any more claim on her attention than the other, but because she did not choose to be watched.

Besides this, Mrs. Bellingham did not care for music; after she had recognised her different friends round the house, by a nod and a grunt, peculiar to herself, she generally sank into a doze, and said to the nearest person,

" Wake me when the ballet begins."

" Rather an immoral taste for a lady of your time of life," said Theresa, the first time she heard this order expressed, and Mrs. Bellingham was so angry at its being considered so, that she kept the best eye open, nearly throughout the opera.

A few days only, now remained of the residence of Mark and his wife in Hill Street, when suddenly Mrs. Dering arrived in Town.

Her visit was totally unexpected, even by her daughter, but she said it was on urgent business, so no one questioned what it was. She had succeeded in coming over with some friends, and thus getting a free passage and journey as well, for the deluded people upon whose compassionate feelings she had so successfully worked, brought her to Mrs. Chetwode's very door, and as she said she could only remain two nights, she humbly petitioned her dear Theresa's mother-in-law, to allow her to sleep on the sofa in the back drawing-room, during that brief sojourn.

The consequence was, a total rout of a whole household, in order to accommodate Mrs. Dering, and she was installed into a bed-room without any apparent difficulty.

To Theresa, though several months had elapsed since she had seen her mother, her

appearance at that moment was singularly inopportune, for she knew her well enough to.
be certain, that some very imperative necessity
must have brought her over, and she suspected
that it would prove to be—money!

In addition to this, the kindness, the uniform
affection, and consideration, of both Mrs.
Chetwode and Marian to the young wife, during
her stay with them, had, towards the close of
her visit, wrought on her feelings sufficiently
to awake in her, something like repentance for
having taken all the attentions as though they
were her right, and given but little in return,
and she had wished—during that week at least
— to devote herself to them, and leave an
agreeable impression, at least on them, if on
no one else, behind her.

The *bruyante* presence therefore, of her restless and excitable mother, would effectually
divert her from this laudable intention, and
when they were shut up together in cabinet
council, Theresa rather impatiently enquired,

what could have brought her to England just as she and Mr. Chetwode were leaving town.

"You shall see," was all Mrs. Dering said, but from the voluminous folds of her dress, in every gigantic plait of which, there appeared to be a pocket for the reception of articles of every degree of magnitude, she soon produced a reply as satisfactory, as any words could be.

A handful of papers, some small, but mostly long, narrow, and delicately lined with blue, emerged from the depths, and laying them down, one by one, in a file, on the table, she exclaimed—

"Now you will guess what brought me over!"

The very sight of these papers, which Theresa saw in a moment were every one of them bills, hardened her heart, and leaning back in her chair with that face of desperate determination which she knew so well how to assume, she said in the coldest of voices,

" Thank Heaven, nothing in which *I* have any concern, for I did not leave a single bill in Paris."

" No, my dear—not in Paris I allow ;—these little accounts have nothing whatever to do with Paris—they are small debts contracted by you in England."

" In England ?" repeated Theresa in amazement, " what can you mean ?—Mr. Chetwode was so exceedingly generous to me abroad, that before I employed any dressmaker in Town, I made an arrangement, that my bills of this year should not come in till next; how then can you possibly call them, ' bills contracted by me in England ?' "

The faintest tinge of colour rose to Mrs. Dering's nose ;—additional colour, for her blushes seemed never to patronise her cheeks, but preferred going where the tint that should have animated *them*, was now established permanently ;

" Not since your marriage, my darling —I do

not mean since your marriage—I mean *before.*"

It was now Theresa's turn to blush, and the rich red hue that dyed cheek, and brow, and throat, showed her mother that prosperity had refined her feelings, and that a difficult task was before her.

But the mother had less delicacy than the daughter; she did not respect the feelings of shame which thus spoke in Theresa's face, and choked her very utterance ; she rattled on, indifferent to the scorn which was settling on the countenance of her child, and explained to her, with the most fluent effrontery, that the bills which she had brought over with her, and which she insinuated that Theresa must pay, were contracted at the different expensive shops in town, at which the *trousseau* of Theresa had been procured !

In silence Theresa listened —in silence she overlooked them, and then, when each had been carefully examined, she exclaimed,

"Mamma, I do wonder you are not ashamed!"

The sentence was an outburst of earnest and honest, indignation thrown, as it were, from her curling lips, with all the fervency of the most utter contempt, but it failed to make due impression on one, whom a life of similar acts, had rendered callous to public opinion.

Mrs. Dering, on the contrary, laughed; she actually laughed, and said,

"Oh, Theresa, marriage *has* altered you!"

And Theresa, still glowing with vexation, gave vent to a torrent of reproaches.

"How you can possibly come here, Mamma! —here, where even I, am but a guest!—how you can come with that array of bills—bills contracted by you, without, I fear, the slightest intention on your part of ever paying them yourself, surpasses my comprehension!—well do I recollect in our young days, the many ways and means we resorted to, when such odious letters as these came upon us, but never, never, Mother, have you yet stooped to anything like shis!"

My dearest Theresa!" protested Mrs. Dering, "you are dreaming!—count these bills up once more—see the the sum to which they amount —how could you ever have imagined that out of my small means I could have paid them myself?"

"I *did* imagine it," retorted her daughter, "and I expected it too; I little thought I should ever have the humiliation of asking my husband to pay for the very clothes in which he married me!"

"Of course I do not expect you to say any-thing to Mr. Chetwode," said Mrs. Dering hastily — "surely with your handsome pin-money......"

"With that, Mamma, you have nothing to do—you do not know my resources, nor my expenses;—only tell me, how is it you cannot defray these bills?"

"Because I never intended," said the mother,

determined not thus to be put down by her child—" I told you before you were married that if I gave you a *trousseau* such as Mr. Chetwode's wife should have, it was not in my power to pay for it—so here are the bills— you must remember my writing that to you, down at Tunbridge Wells."

Theresa considered a moment, and then she had a faint recollection of some letter, saying something about Mr. Keating's insisting on having no bills, and Mrs. Dering's resolution to manage better when it came to Theresa's turn. This she did remember—but she had never dreamt that the sentence, " manage better when it came to Theresa's turn" bore this signification.

" And really and truly you cannot pay them ?" she said.

" I cannot ; they amount to nearly half my yearly income, and I lived on cheeseparings, to pay for what Georgy had on her marriage, which was not nearly so much as I bestowed on you."

"Bestowed!" repeated Theresa, in a contemptuous murmur, "a very inappropriate term, mother!"

"It looks very much as if you will *make* me bestow them, "retorted Mrs. Dering, angry in her turn, and inwardly terrified lest Theresa or her husband should decidedly refuse her request—"I tell you honestly Theresa, if Clémence had not written me a most impertinent and threatening letter, I never would have put myself in this abject position;"

Theresa's pride, not her heart, was touched, and she gathered up the papers.

"Not a word more," said she, "not a syllable farther, on so odious a subject; I will take the only course which my duty suggests, and that is, I will place these accounts in the hands of my husband..."

"You will ruin me!" cried Mrs. Dering, "you certainly are mad, Theresa! — expose me to Mr. Chetwode, when the sole reason that incited me to the extravagance, was love for you, and pride in your appearance?"

"All the more likely that you will be forgiven," returned Theresa—"at all events that is the only course I choose to pursue;—the bills amount to £215—I will not stop to enquire of you if *I* had the lilac *glacé* silk dress charged by Clémence at eleven guineas—nor this white capote and feathers—nor this *pélerine* of richest blondes—nor a *mantelet de velours*—nor several other items which certainly never formed part of *my trouseau*—do not speak, mamma! it only makes matters worse"—and suddenly seizing the papers, Theresa darted out of the room.

Mrs. Dering had not expected her to wind up the conversation in this abrupt manner, and she sat trembling in that quiet little room by herself, alike alarmed at her position, and at the probable refusal which Mr. Chetwode might give, to aiding and abetting her, in what she considered to be the most clever thing she had ever done.

At last, Theresa returned, and her hands, instead of holding the expected cheque, were empty.

Mrs. Dering nearly dropped; but at last her daughter spoke.

"He will pay them, mamma—he has them all ready to settle this afternoon. One thing only he insisted on, and that was, that he should do it himself, and he begged me to tell you, as delicately as I could, that never from this hour——"

"I know—I know," interrupted Mrs. Dering nervously; "not to do it again you mean. Yes—yes; but I have no more daughters, thank goodness. Was he angry, my dearest?"

"Why ask?" said Theresa bitterly. "Since he has promised to save your credit, and pay the bills, what care you whether he were angry or not? No, mother; but remember, the next time you come to England on such an errand, do not come here."

Back to Paris, then, as fast as ever she could go, did Mrs. Dering wend her way, lowered in the sight of all who knew the errand, on which she came over.

In Mrs. Chetwode's opinion, she was irrecoverably. lost—for to his mother, Mark had confided the simple facts, in order to benefit by her advice, and she had recommended him to accede, for this once, to the demand, on the understanding that it was never again to be repeated.

Her departure was the greatest relief in the world to Theresa. The day she left Hill-street happened to be a Tuesday—Theresa's last opera-night—and though they were to leave town the next day, the relief from Mrs. Dering's presence lightened her spirits, and made her feel cheerful and happy.

She did all sorts of amiable things; took

Marian out in the carriage with her; asked Mrs. Bellingham to accept a seat in her box again that evening, and left a note at the club for Mr. Bathurst, saying she had a place for him too, if he liked to avail himself of it.

He was disengaged and accepted, and they all sat down together at dinner for the last time.

Mark was silent and low; he could hardly touch his dinner, nor utter a syllable; and a general feeling of depression seemed to pervade all the party, excepting Theresa.

For her part, she could not, even to herself, account for her elated spirits that night; she even tried to moderate them, and succeeded, yet her heart felt lighter than it had done for a long time, and an unaccountable joyousness made the effort to appear of the humour of those around her, quite painful.

At last, they started for the opera, and the restraint she had imposed upon herself was removed; she talked and laughed, like the gay and giddy Theresa Dering of other days, and the broad *bandeau* of diamonds round her forehead, hardly sparkled more than those lustrous eyes.

Mr. Bathurst owned to himself that evening, for the first time, that she was fascinating, and no longer wondered at the power she possessed over his friend.

That night, the eternal Don Giovanni was performed, and Theresa, knowing every note of it by heart, had not been particularly interested; she had talked till she was quite tired, and towards the end of the opera, she leant her head back against the dingy draperies, and looked round at the brilliant circle, with something of regret to think that she was leaving town thus early in the season—for it was now the middle of May.

Mrs. Bellingham was dozing; she had expressed the customary wish, to be roused before the ballet began, and Mark and his friend were quite at the back of the box, deep in conversa-

tion, when, as Theresa's eyes descended to the
level of the pit, and wandered amongst the mass
of dark heads congregated there, her careless
glances were suddenly arrested, by an object
standing amongst the hundreds of indifferent
people—by a countenance, which, once seen, was
not likely to be forgotten, and which, the
instant it met Theresa's observation, stood out
as it were, in relief, from the dark mass, and
fixed her attention, without leaving her even
power to remove it.

Spell-bound, she looked, and looked again,
at that face, on which was neither smile nor
faintest token of recognition, yet the glance
gave back her own as fixedly, and as unflinch-
ingly. She could not be mistaken; she felt
certain who it was. Her heart beat almost
audibly, and shorter and shorter she drew her
breath, for there—before her—returning her
steady gaze, without one look to say she was
either remembered, forgiven, or recognised,
stood Edward Sydenham.

At first, he did not move a muscle—it almost seemed as if he did not breathe—but suddenly, just as the lights had begun dancing and flickering in her eyes, and a sound like the rushing of water almost deafened her, she saw him raise his hand—in it were opera-glasses, and as he was carrying them to his eyes apparently with the intention of fixing them upon herself, a mist spread itself before her sight, she half rose from her seat, and when, a few moments afterwards, she found herself in a distant chair, she neither knew how she had got there, or whether the scene she had so nearly made, had been observed. Mrs. Bellingham was awaking, and looking about her with heavy eyelids, yet that manner which people put on when they wish others to think they have not been to sleep; and Mark and his ally, were still deep in a railroad discussion.

"Why did Mrs. Mark go home?" was Mrs. Bellingham's incoherent question, not seeing her opposite neighbour in her place, and fancying she should prove her acute sense of all that had been passing, by some such hazardous sentence, and the *sotto voce* answer "I am here," was the first intimation Chetwode had, of his wife's change of place.

When he looked at her, he was alarmed at the colour she had turned ; she seemed shivering with cold, too—and unable to glean from her, whether she were well or ill, he asked her if she would like to go home.

"Yes—home, by all means," and to the infinite surprise of Mrs. Bellingham, who had never before been treated as a cipher, Mr. Bathurst was left in charge of the old lady, and Mark and his wife passed through the desolate crush-room, and down the deserted stair-case, and went their way, home.

In their transit they had met no one, they had seen no one, and the impression on Theresa's mind was, that she had been dreaming ; her recollection of the shock she had received, became at last, of that vague, indefinite description which characterizes a startling, truthful dream, and painful as the waking to a sense of delusion was, still she was half glad to persuade herself into the idea, that she had not seen Edward Sydenham again ; from the very day of her marriage she had looked forward to that meeting with dread, yet, had it actually taken place, perhaps she would have rejoiced in all thankfulness, to think that it was over ;— and this she called, forgetting him !

END OF VOL. II.

T. C. NEWBY, Printer, 72, Mortimer St., Cavendish Sq.

January, 1848.

Mr. Newby has just Published,

I

Mrs. CROWE'S New work

In 2 Vols,

THE NIGHT SIDE OF NATURE;

OR, GHOSTS OF GHOST SEERS.

By the author of " Susan Hopley." " Lilly Dawson."

II

In 3 Vols.

TREACHERY.

A NOVEL.

III

In 3 Vols.

THE COUNT; OR SUBLUNARY LIFE.

A NOVEL

By one in a High Station

IV.

THE RUSSIAN SKETCH BOOK.

By IVAN GOLOVIE.

Author of " Russia under Nicholas I."

V.

In 3 Vols.
DAUGHTERS.
By the Author of " The Gambler's Wife." &c,

VI.

In 3 Vols. *(Second Edition.)*
THE CARDINAL'S DAUGHTER.
By the Author of " The Scottish Heiress." &c.

VII.

In 3 Vols.
JEREMIAH PARKES.
By the Author of " The Poor Cousin."

VIII.

In 3 Vols.
ALL CLASSES.
By the Author of " The Ward of the Crown."

IX.

In 3 Vols.
JACK ARIEL.
By the Author of " The Post Captain."

X.

In 3 Vols.
CROMWELL IN IRELAND.

WS - #0038 - 031221 - C0 - 229/152/20 - PB - 9781330571378 - Gloss Lamination